Lover's Salvation

Book Two The Hemocil Society

Ruthie L Manier

Other Books By Ruthie L Manier
The Hemocil Society Series
Lover's Curse – Book One – Spring 2014
Lover's Salvation – Book Two – Summer 2015
Lover's Refuge – Book Three – Coming Winter 2015

Please keep your eyes open for Lover's Refuge the third book in The Hemocil Society Series.
Coming Winter 2015.

Acknowledgements

Jon ...You are my soul mate the man that stands next to me no matter what I choose to do. You're my special place I go to that non-other can share, and I love you for the serenity that brings.

Sister Teresa, thank you from the bottom of my heart for reading my manuscript every-time I made revisions. I owe you big time little sister!

To all my friends and co-workers at United General Hospital you are my inspiration. I appreciate every single one of you.

Last but not least my graphic designer M.S. Fowle I am so grateful that my friend Tara Ellis introduced me to your work. It's amazing! My cover is alluring to say the least, and I love it.

Table of Contents

Acknowledgements iii

Facts About The Hemocil Society vii

Stupid Car 1

The Cabin 17

Snooping 30

Witch Hunters 40

New Beginning 46

The Clan 56

The Witch 64

Memories 79

Town 86

Receiving Angel 96

Staked 102

Running 105

Saved 112

The Shitkick Bar 117

Date 124

Forgiving 134

Angel of Suicide 143

Reconnecting 154

Men 159

Destroying The Enemy 172

Happy Endings 189

About the Author 197

Facts About The Hemocil Society

The term Hemocil refers to a blood pill. Hemo means blood and cil is in reference to cell, as in blood cell. The Blood pill is used to replace the need for blood so that vampires would not turn to savages and would be able to live a "human-like" existence with perks and drawbacks to each lifestyle.

Vampires taking the pill are called Va'atacos and vampires who refuse the pill are called Suntanic. The Suntanics are usually vile creatures and are not allowed within the city limits unless they possess a special pass which is only given to people of law enforcement, military, or vampires working for the state who need one hundred percent of their powers to do their jobs. There are a few other special conditions in which a Suntanic is allowed to roam within city limits.

To prove they are Va'atacos and to continue living within the city limits vampires are required to partake in random blood tests, and must go to ground for rejuvenation once a month where they are locked in until their allotted time is up. The penalty for not following these rules is sometimes death...

1

Stupid Car

Issy

I stumble into the Shitkick Bar out of the sweltering Washington heat. A hundred and twenty degrees is hot anywhere, but for Skagit County these temperatures are record breaking. My clothes are soaked from the sweat clinging to every inch of my skin. The moisture started at the base of my scalp, saturating my hair trickling down my face and into my eyes. Exhausted, I fall against the inside of the door as it slowly shuts behind me. I catch the breeze almost immediately from the vent above my head, and it feels so damn good.

I close my eyes clearing my vision while singing out a ceremonial, "Hallelujah," literally voicing the words out loud in thanks to God in heaven I made it out of the blistering heat into the salvation of air conditioning.

I can't believe my stupid car broke down again; this has to be about the tenth time this year, if only I could afford to buy a new one. What am I gonna do this time? I possess no money to get my car fixed. And the posse is close. Too close. Why, oh why does everything tend to be so damned hard? But that's how I got into this sad predicament in the first place - running from the hunters!

Unable to motivate myself to move any further I relax a minute leaning against the door as the coolness sifts through every pore of my body. Breathing in, deep full cool breaths... in and out... in and out. Um, the fan begins to revive me; I could stand here all day and I might until the next patron tries to enter the door, I think with a long drawn out sigh.

A second later I get a prickling sensation down my spine and through my shoulder's as though a cackle of hungry hyenas watched my every move; detecting how eerily quiet the room is I grudgingly open my eyes. Focusing with a couple of blinks I see the place is completely packed. I gasp! I must be weaker than I thought. Incapable of moving, as if an invisible force of some kind is holding me in tack. Everyone in the room customers and the employees alike are silent gaping at me. My feet are heavy as if set in blocks of concrete, my backside a huge magnet drawing me towards the door and my stomach is swirling. Ugh! I hope I don't puke in front of all these people.

"Get the lady a drink - quick, before she croaks." A man with an accent calls out, "She definitely earned one having the nerve to walk in here looking like that!"

I inhale as my eyes widen briefly and directly afterwards my butt hits the floor. Ouch, that smarted is all I can think before everything goes black. I seem to lose consciousness my mind slipping in and out and I can't help, but recall the last time it wheeled this out of control, the time when I had mistakenly drank homebrew thinking it was mortal alcohol. Vampire hooch - made for vampires only who like the hard stuff. I can't focus. Not good. Not good at all. Just breathe. Stay calm. I mustn't let her take over.

"Leave her alone Buck, can't you tell she's in need of assistance. Poor thing probably acquired a sun stroke walking around outside in this heat. Come help me get her up and onto a bar stool."

"I didn't mean her any harm; I was trying to lighten the air. You saw everybody staring at her with mouths watering, as though she was a snack.

I thought I was doing the woman a favor warning her that the room was full."

Within seconds I identify the sound of high heels followed by boots clicking towards me. I strain to sit up straight, but my limbs are so heavy. I open and close my eyes to clear my vision, but my eyes are clouded at best. I try to speak, but it's as though someone hit the mute button and nothing comes out. I need blood or a supplement now. I ran out of my Hemocil days ago. Not good. My fear is if I don't get some form of nourishment soon, I'm going to turn into a bitch vampire from hell and this particular vamps hidden power holds the potential to destroy us all.

"Oh Buck, really...just shush!" The woman scolds as they walk towards me. She sounds really friendly so I don't think I need to worry about being man handled in anyway.

I must be the only immortal on earth with stress related problems I think trying not to roll myself up in a little ball, but who wouldn't - with the super human abilities I carry inside me. Frightening stuff, I think practicing my breathing technique in and out - long - slow - breaths. I don't imagine I'll be able to deal with my pill issue here; seriously, if I don't get one soon, though, I'm afraid I might attack someone. And I think Buck, sounds like a perfect candidate. Besides, I don't like being this vulnerable in a room full of people. I work at slowing my aspirations down. In through my nose and out through the lips deep long breaths.

"What...I thought laughter would help," The rude man pleas to the woman. Boy is he wrapped around her little finger, can we say whipped. But I will admit he sounds irritatingly decent like he possesses some remorse for embarrassing me, or more like - he hasn't a clue. Stupid man! This only succeeds in ticking me off a little more because frankly I'm not ready to forgive him quite yet.

"Buck, it didn't help. You embarrassed her." Sophia says as their footsteps stop right beside me.

"Okay folks the shows all over," A man in the back ground exclaims before the sweet sound of Bad Moon Rising from the jute box fills the air and I am so thankful hopefully the distraction will take some of the attention off me. The familiar noise of balls sliding through a pool table and a voice saying, "I play winner," tells me the music's worked as others around the room begin to talk too.

When I gather the strength to open my eyes, a beautiful dark haired green eyed woman probably near her late forties is leaning over me looking concerned. She smiles then turns away and calls to the bartender, "bring the house special." She holds her hand down for me to grab on as the man, I'm assuming the man behind her is Buck, takes hold of my other hand and they help me to my feet using their spare hands to stabilize me. I want to growl at the Jerk.

"My name is Sophia, this here's Buck, my Eternalmate," she leans closer and in a hush tone confides, "He doesn't always think before he speaks," she winks at me flashes her eyes towards him, shaking her head and rolling her eyes back to me, "we own this establishment." She adds. I detect even though she's reprimanding him the love they share for one another is unmistakable. The kind of passion I hope I find someday.

Surprisingly my new rival is a strikingly handsome man and appears to be around Sophia's age with black hair and eyes almost as dark. He is a huge man the size of a grizzly bear. Not fat by any means, the man is tall wide and full of pure muscle. These two were both turned later in life and I can only guess it wasn't by choice, but there's one thing for certain they took real good care of themselves before.

He smiles reaching for my hand.

I stiffen. I don't think so buddy.

"See Buck, The woman doesn't trust you enough to shake your hand." Sophia says, looking at him before her eyes turn to me and she adds, "Believe me honey, he doesn't bite, innocents."

"Ahh hell, forgive me miss," He says running his fingers over his short black head.

"I meant no harm. My woman is correct, I was thoughtless. How may I make things right?" he asks looking slightly embarrassed.

His apology is sincere, so I decide Sophia's right and he didn't think before speaking. I will give him one more chance, before judging him the big jerk I thought he was. Besides the more I eyeball him he seems more like a teddy bear, although I bet he could be a badass if he needs to be. They both hold on to me for a moment longer to make sure I'm stable before releasing my hands again.

"Hi," I croak out surprised by the harsh sound of my own voice. I intake a long breath licking my dry lips before continuing, "I'm Esmeralda, but please call me Issy." I turn my full attention to him and add, "If you want to redeem yourself I'm in bad need of something real strong." The couple faces each other and I spot the concerned expressions probably having a private chat using the Eternalmate only line. Just breathe.

"Sure, no problem." Buck says with a knowing gleam to his eyes before turning his body slightly making room for the person walking up. "As a matter of fact here the goods are now."

That's when I see the man from behind him. I blink a couple of times thinking I'm seeing things - a mirage probably from too much sun and no blood or I've died and gone to heaven - nope, my eyes are fine. Buck wasn't kidding. The so called bartender would put any Greek God to shame and I think Thor's been replaced on my private top ten list of sexiest men ever. He carries a glass of water in one hand and a shot of some kind of sup in the other, causing my mouth to automatically water and I'm not quite sure if it's because of the man, or the blood.

At the sight of this 'God,' my butt almost hit's the floor again. Damn - I'm weak. My body is shutting down my movement slow and strained my head drawing circles within my brain. Somehow the man sets the drink down on a nearby table reaching his strong arms out and catching me before I land. My air catches at his touch. He lifts me up into his strong able arms cradling my form close almost protectively to his hard chest, and carries me towards the closest bar stool. His aroma fills my nostrils and my head swims; simply breathing him in. Sandalwood and Old Spice, umm... I hate this about myself, but I love that fragrance. I don't want him to release me, which is odd; I normally don't like to be touched.

"Did she pass out?" The woman asks with true concern in her voice.

"Nope, she's real close though." Buck says. "From the looks of her she's real low on blood and been out in the sun considerably too long."

"Yeah that was my thought. We need to get fluids in her pronto." says the man holding me and I love the way his accented voice is so deep low and soothing.

"Should we take her in the back and start a line on her?" asks Buck.

"Nope, we'll only poke her if that's the last resort. Let's try the special stuff first and see if we can get her to hold it down." Answers the man again. "Here you go, I'm going to put it to your lips now and I need you to try and drink it slowly. Shake your head if you understand."

I shake my head and a split second later the glass touches my mouth. I suck some in and almost choke. He pulls the shot away from my lips.

"Woman, what part of drink slow don't you get?"

"More." I croak out.

"Give it a minute to settle." He says in a hiss.

All of a sudden I get a whiff of something else, ewe, and it's not the man. Oh please lord, say this isn't happening. A second later my mind registers the fact the stench is coming from me. I force my lids open and glance down at my dirty wardrobe and spot the sweat stains on the more private parts. My breasts, my arm pits...oh no - not there - my crotch. I stiffen, oh my God. I stink. Not to mention I'm probably getting this beautiful man all wet, gross. I try to wiggle out of his arms, but he holds on tighter. Tears threaten to fill my eyes and I want to disappear. Why do these kinds of things always happen to me? I think mortified.

"I got you. Take deep, slow; breaths and you'll be fine. We've got some more of the special drink; I'll give you in a minute which should jump start your system, and fix you right up in no time. You're safe with me," The God purrs in a baritone husky hum near my right ear his chest so hard to my breast causing me to shiver and shamefully and terribly inappropriately my nipples automatically harden, his voice reminding me of the old blues for some reason. His breath fluttering across my skin like butterfly kisses. Does this Supreme Being realize I'm trying not to go into a full blown panic attack?

"Is the air conditioning on to high?" he asks as I try to open my eyes back up.

I lift my gaze up to his shocked and afraid; he's talking about my over sensitive nipples and am taken back.

My mouth flies wide open. My lids open and shut trying to make sure if what I'm seeing is for real. Surprisingly enough they are and now I can't turn away to save my life. Startling colors of crystal sky blue eyes are gazing back into mine. They can't be natural. I silently wonder if he's wearing some kind of new contact. One thing is for sure I couldn't avert my eyes if I wanted to. His are hypnotic. Help me I'm falling. They appear as though stars from the skies above fell into them landing directly in the precise spot to make them perfectly unique, and they're sparkling at me now. *Twinkle, twinkle*, I think delirious drinking them in. I should turn my eyes away, but oddly enough I can't.

Besides the better question is why he isn't? His eyes are mesmerizing, heated. I'm lost in them my thoughts spiraling out in circles within my head. Just breathe.

Than the truth slaps me in the face - The vamp is hypnotizing me!

Before I can avert my eyes from his he smiles and my world halts on its axis. A roomful of people vanish. Still he searches my eyes. I melt inside my eyelashes at half-mast my head still spinning within. I am bewitched and there is not a damn thing I can do. Sadly his face changes and the smile is soon replaced with a firm jaw as he clears his throat..

"Woman, what were you thinking walking out side on a day like today? Are you not aware the thermostat reads a hundred and twenty degrees?" He scolds setting me on a bar stool still searching my eyes and I get the impression he thinks I'm missing a screw.

I nod yes, what else could I do. Of course I realize how hot the weather is out there. I manage to flash my eyes away from his long enough to do a quick survey of my tank top and jeans again. Hello. I'm covered in sweat. Still I miss his touch immediately. Not to mention the assurance his arms wrapped snugly around my waist gave me for those brief few minutes. Last time I had Security like that was my mom and papa's arms folded around me. When they were alive even the scariest of times barely affected me, and why should it they always took care of things, but I avoid thinking about them for the memories of losing my parents sadden me. I reflect a century was a long time ago. My lips curl up resulting in a childish pout and I am surprised at my own reaction. Just breathe.

Remembering how sweaty my clothes are my eyes quickly inspect his shirt. Thank the Gods he was spared. I set my hand to my chest relieved.

A second later my eyes flash to his as he hands me the rest of the special blood drink and I realize by his arched brow he's actually expecting an answer to the silly weather question. "Here, drink this one slow you're not getting another one for fifteen minutes." He says the problem is his smooth like southern Irish whiskey voice turned my brain to mush. I'm having problems with my thinking process besides able to get my vocal chords to articulate the right words. My mouth is so dry. Walk? Was I walking? Come on Issy speak, I repeat in my head. Stop acting like a damn fool-speak! The man will think you're daft!

Meanwhile Sophia walks up and starts talking to Marcus taking the attention from me. Somewhere in my outer realm I hear her ask, "How's she doing?" As he turns his head her way I am released from his spell and can breathe again.

"Hard to say she's still real low on blood and a little spacey because of it, I think, but a few more pints and some rest will hopefully do the trick.

"You don't think we need to take her to the clinic in Mount Vernon?" asks Sophia.

"Nope; I recon we should keep a close eye on her here for a while and see if the treatment works." Marcus answers her and all I can think is you're damn right I'm not going to a clinic even though it's exactly the place I want to go. But the Va'atacos clinics and urgent Cares are the first place the posse will search.

I shoot down the lifeblood practically licking the glass wanting each drop, while they finish speaking about me as though I'm not here beside them listening to every word. I am so grateful for the offering and a moment to gather my scattered thoughts. Hopefully the sup will help, but I'm so dehydrated I crave more.

"Okay, but make certain to only give her the mixture approximately every twenty minutes." says Sophia over her shoulder walking to the other end of the counter to wait on another patron.

"Yes mother." he retorts teasingly as he turns his head back towards me with a questioning brow, a beer in his right hand and a glass of what I can only surmise as blood supplement wine in the other. I smile lick my lips and shake my head up and down. Quite sure I resemble a puppy waiting for its master to give him a steak bone. It took all the strength I could muster not to let my tongue hang out of my mouth.

Truthfully I'm beyond the point of caring. I need as much blood as I can get, period. The nourishment he gave me helped considerably, but I face the truth. I can't be out of my Hemocil any longer. If I don't get one today by tomorrow or the next day I'll be changing into a Suntanic like it or not. He sets the wine before me and the beer on a coaster to the left of me. He spots my empty shot glass and clucks his tongue a couple of times shaking his head.

"You were supposed to sip the special drink."

I grin and my eyes follow his movements curiously as he walks around the bar and sits down right next to me before answering his question. Hmm, must be his break time, is all I can guess.

"I was working on my tan of course."

His head snaps up. Shocked angry blue eyes drill into mine, "Is that supposed to be a joke?"

"Well, yes." I say confused. Why is he so upset?

"You barely made it through the front door." He points at the door in question. "I don't think the fact you almost died today is a laughing matter. You should take better precautions with your life, woman. Just because the Hemocil allows us to go out in the sun doesn't mean you should play with fire." Jeez he sounds like my father used to sound.

"Lighten up, it's all good. I made it." *What does he care?*

He clears his throat. "You mean - barely made it."

"Fine, it was a close call. Are you happy now?" He stares at me for a minute with a stone hard face firm jaw lips sealed before I spot a muscle jump in his cheek and he relaxes.

"What happened? You don't appear to be a complete moron to me so did you run out of gas? Did you fight with a boyfriend and him leave you by the roadside, or what possessed you to be outside walking around?"

"Well thanks ... I think. You're assumption is close, except the 'boy-friend' part. No "boyfriend" I use quote signs. My car broke down a few miles out of town," I say reaching for my drink. Picking up the wine glass I start to gulp it down like I had the shot, but before the liquid touches my mouth he grasps on to the end of the goblet. He is trying to pull it out of my hand while I grasp on tighter, but I am weak and my strength is no match for his. The growl starts in my belly low and beastly then shoots through my chest and almost out, but he stopped me with one look - the perfect one, my heart skips double time, his right brow arched, intense daring blue eyes staring into mine, mouth pursed up to the side. Umm, such sweet determined lips causing me to yearn for a kiss even while wanting to chastise this man for grabbing my blood. What kind of spell is this?

"Shh, calm yourself. If you guzzle it fast which is obviously your intent you're going to get sick. No doubt about it. Your choice of course," he adds letting go of the glass. "If I were you I'd take small sips." he says in his slow deep soothing hum causing a quiver to slide over my flesh, his sexy eyes still burning through mine. Just breathe.

"Oh, right, makes since." I say my feathers still a little ruffled. Who does he think he is? I am a Va'atacos woman and can take care of myself, yet still it's surprisingly sweet for this man to act like he cares. I realize as he arches his brow at me again he's still waiting for the rest of my story. I can hardly breathe besides think, he is so overwhelmingly man.

"Anyways, excuse my disruption, will you please continue."

"Well there's not much more to say. I waited over an hour hoping somebody would drive by, but my luck no one did, and by that time the sun was already beginning to sting my skin. So I figured if I didn't want to die a horrific death ...I had to walk fast. I had no other choice."

"Hmm, which highway were you driving on?"

"I'm not sure."

He clears his throat.

The problem is I can't tell this stranger the truth. My only option had been to travel by foot for miles down an old abandoned road because that's the breaks for a person on the run who is forced to use only back roads. I grimace. Stupid hunters! Unfortunately for me this particular path had zero greenery to shade me from the rays! This sucked because everywhere else my eyes strayed were plenty of trees. Hello western Washington home of the evergreen. I bet it's the only stretch on this side of the state without them.

"You don't remember the name of the highway you were on?"

"Nope, I'm not from Skagit County, only passing through. But don't worry I sketched a road-map of where I left my VW in my head." I add grinning tapping my index finger to my temple.

"Ok." he says chuckling. "I was just curious because I can't imagine a highway around here so baron, the traffic was nonexistence for over an hour? Could be the heats keeping folks at home."

"Yeah, I bet you're right. I'll tell you what the blinking neon sign outside reading," I use quote signs; 'The Shitkick Bar,' was my salvation."

"I could tell by your entrance," he says giving me a curious yet concerned examination; "Well I'm glad you found us. Most places in town closed early today due to the heat."

I nod. "That's two of us. I'm not surprised about businesses' closing today, it's so hot out there towards the end of my journey I actually visualized myself dead lying on the road, with the scorching rays so hot burning me alive... while I writhe in pain and agony. I imagined my skin melting from my bones. My ashes sifting down into the cracks and crevices of the concrete, and back into the soil from whence they came. Ugh, I get the heebie geebies at the memory." He stares at me for a minute with a blank countenance and I'm thinking Opps, TMI.

"Hmm, a bit morbid." He makes a scrunched up grossed out face before adding dryly. "It sounds like luck was on your side after all."

"Luck?"

"You're here aren't you?" He retorts. I give a half-wit smile reaching my hand out and grasping my wine. He scowls at me and I swear I received his words loud and clear 'Sips only,' even though he didn't open his mouth.

"Yes father." I say in the same way he had teased Sophia earlier. Taking a small sip I cherish the bitter sweetness before swallowing. I lick my lips again not wanting to miss even a drop. My body starts to revive as I sense his eyes are still assessing me.

My tongue darts out to the top of my lip and back. I glance up from below lashes to catch his eyes staring at my mouth like he is over come with hunger and wants to devour them. A rapid spark ignites low in my belly. So heated the small flame spreads through my blood like a raging fire out of control. My eyes dart away from his afraid of the way he is affecting me. My breath catches and my heart sputters, my palms sweaty. Just breathe.

"I'll take you to your car and fix it for you if it's possible."

My eyes snap back up to his. "Excuse me?"

"Well you need your wheels don't you?"

"Yes, of course, but?"

"It's settled. By the way what was it doing before breaking down?" He adds. Ignoring me as if I don't affect him one bit yet he stripped me bear with unfamiliar emotions. Why would this bartender help me? We've never even met before.

"Hmm, let me think." I answer as I see a loud drunken mortal woman two tables down starting a little ruckus with another woman at the table across from her, but I'm not sure if she's only mortal or not it's hard to get a reading with so many people in one room.

I chance a peek at my handsome bartender. He is now watching the action too as Buck, walks over and tries settling drunken lady down.

This man is hot, silky long black hair held back by a strap of leather at his nape. A rather nasty scar which strangely only adds to his sex appeal on the right side of his neck and I wonder what caused the disfigurement. A terrible battle I presume because it takes a Hell of a lot for a vampire's skin to mar. More than likely means he wasn't able to get to blood and go to ground to heal properly. Too bad I'll never be told the real story.

I continue my inspection a sexy aristocratic shaped face, full sensual lips 'any girl in her right mind would die for one kiss.' Tall - probably 6'3, wide powerful shoulders and long muscular arms - welcoming ones the kind having them wrapped around you would make you feel safer than ever before. Anyway I liked the security of them. My adrenaline begins to race remembering the warmth of them holding me a few minutes ago. Slim rippled long waist attached to small squared hips and strong long legs. My eyes slip back to his and I can tell by his sultry smile he likes the way I worshiped his body. Officially embarrassed I move my head back to the commotion as Buck is leading drunken female and her male friend out of the bar in a hypnotized state. Just breathe.

He cleared his throat yet again, reminding me he's waiting for my reenactment. I try timidly to describe the best I can. "It ahh sputtered... made a weird loud popping sound... steam spilled out of the hood from all sides blocking my view to where I couldn't drive."

My car is my home, literally. It's my way of life since I was little more than a child over a hundred years ago. Not wanting to linger on my past now I turn my attention back to the sexy bartender. The man who's got me all steamed up and I can only hope he is oblivious to the fact.

"Hmm, probably the radiator."

"Oh no, radiator sounds expensive, and I'm embarrassed to say my wallets seen better days. May I pay you for your services later after I've had time to thicken it? Or if you'd rather I could work the money off some-how...perhaps umm - dishes?" I only met this Godly appearing immortal an few minutes ago, but he's my only hope right now. There's no choice, however to trust him.

Most of the time I make my living by reading peoples tarot cards, but I'm almost positive this hunk would scoff if I mentioned such a thing. My aunt taught me the skill when I was a young girl to read peoples futures when my mom wasn't paying attention. She said the skill could come in handy for me one day and she was right. She told me I was a natural and predicted I could perform the trick without the cards and she's right about that too. Drunken people in bars are easy to fool and love their future's read. I make my money this way.

Perchance I could do a few here so I can pay him for his work, I think glancing around at the crowd. Next thing I spot is his hand cupping my chin lifting my face up until we're eye to eye once more. I flinch, not used to being touched especially by strangers. An electric current starts to hum from where our skin met. While his mesmerizing eyes grab my complete attention. He calms me in his low hypnotic voice.

"Woman, I only wish to help. I'm good with mechanics and I'll fix your vehicle if it's possible." he shrugs, "If for some unlikely reason it's too screwed up and can't be fixed on the street then I will tow the car to my garage. It might require ordering some parts, not a problem it's a short couple of hours ride to Shucks. Paul the manager will deliver them if I ask him too for a little added fee." My heart melts for the second time today. "My God, woman, what kind of man do you think I am? I said nothing of money and wouldn't take any if you offered." He adds huskily shaking his head back and forth and I spy his strong perfectly sculpted profile. "Please don't insult my character again. I'm sure you would do the same thing for me if I was down on my luck and needed help." He murmurs quietly, eyes serious and I come to the conclusion he would be incensed if I said anything else about money. "Do you understand?"

"Yes, but I did not mean to offend..."

"Shh ...calm yourself, woman."

"But..." he gives me a frosty scowl crossing his arms and I swear I can almost recall my father's voice saying, 'Issy, not one more word on the matter, or else!'

"I don't even know your name?" I manage to whisper looking back up into those stunning sparkling eyes. He melts away all my objections again with a wide endearing smile. My own grin spreads across my face before I can prevent it. I must appear like a little kid being handed a triple scoop ice cream cone. Corny as hell, but I can't seem to stop. His happiness is contagious.

"First we eat and refresh your drink. Next we go to your car. My name pretty woman is Marcus." He gently takes my left hand in his, turning palm side up leaving a feather light kiss to the middle and the tingle shoots all the way to my core. "I'm pleased to make your acquaintance." He purrs star gazing into my eyes.

I gulp and wait for my composure before speaking again.

"Well, umm, same to you Marcus and by the way in case you weren't within ear range earlier when I introduced myself to the owners... I'm

Issy. Thanks, I appreciate your help." I say hoping I don't come off to him as needy as I am. I don't want him to figure out how hard up I am. "But I'm not hungry," I add knowing I can't afford to be splurging what moneys left on bar food. I'll get a blood sup yogurt or a banana later at a bigger grocery store in town. Shopping at a larger one will be loads cheaper and make the difference on whether I eat or not for the next few days.

A smile tugs at his sensuous lips as he says, "The pleasure is all mine." And it causes my lower tummy to quiver with an odd sensation.

"Wait, don't you work here? Is your shift done?" I ask.

His eyebrows shoot up! His head leans back as he laughs a deep hearted all out wonderful from his gut, Santa Claus kind of jolly laugh! I'm stunned. I can't remember ever witnessing such a beautiful sound coming from anyone other than children. I'm in awe. Like a cupids arrow straight to my heart.

"Buck and Sophia are good friends from my homeland. We've recently become reconnected. Neither of us thought are paths would cross again, but by a surprising set of consequences a few years ago we ran smack into each other. They're part of the reason I made the decision to move my cabin here. I check in on them often and help out when I can." He says with laughter still ringing from his voice and his eyes lit up playfully. "I'm here on an extended - much needed vacation."

"Oh!" I retort alarmed, "I'm so sorry; you had brought me the drink so I assumed, well..."

"Calm yourself." Why does he always repeat the same phrase and further more why does Marcus saying those words seem to work like a charm? He takes a long swig off his beer finishing the bottle. Waves Sophia to come over and tips his head to me sobering, jaw firm, eyes intense. "You will eat because quite frankly I don't like to dine alone." he states like I don't get a choice in the matter. He turns his head back to her as she arrives in front of him. He order's for two ignoring what I had said all together and all I can think is where 'did this handsome devil' come from?

Doesn't he realize women of the twenty first century don't like to be told what they will and won't do? I guess because he already ordered and I assume he's planning to pay. Plus, he volunteered to try and fix my car, for - zero none the less. The least I could do is eat with him. I don't want to be rude not to, right? Besides, it's been a couple of days since any real substance touched the inside of my belly and let's face it; free is too good to pass up. I can only hope this man is as trustworthy as he seems, but only time will tell.

2

The Cabin

Awhile later we walk outside as the sun is beginning to set. I smile, glad for the bright rays to be gone. I can't believe I almost died today from it. I always presumed the hunters were my biggest threat. Weird how things like near death experiences snap you back into reality. It doesn't help my blood pills been empty for three days and I need a new script. Not to mention I'm pass due on going to ground by at least two months. I mean how am I supposed to stop at a clinic for the night when I'm constantly running from the posse. My luck the authorities are hunting me with warrants for my arrest, but I never stay in one place long enough for them to catch up with me. Still I worry. If I were to get arrested I'm sure they could get to me, because I don't even think the police can keep me safe from them.

As we pass the corner of the bar he points to his car, "There."

My eyes follow to where he is pointing, "Holy shit what a beaut!" I blurt out because much to my astonishment it's a forest green 1968 Jaguar XJ13. I'm shocked; I laugh thinking the man is joking. I am tickled pink saying, "You wish."

I run to the sporty car not waiting for his response, slowly moving around the Jag worshiping its slick smooth body. Wanting to lay my hands upon its level hard surface, comprehending how rude it would be is the only thing preventing me.

Clearing his throat he walks over to the passenger side of the car reaching in his pocket and pulling out the keys. I gasp and my eyes fly to his as he sticks the key into the lock opening the door. *Ugh, open mouth insert foot. Will I ever learn to zip it?*

Marcus is wealthy and a class act because these babies don't come cheap. Most guys don't own classics unless they're filthy rich, or restored them because it's their thing they like to do. At least this is a good sign he can probably fix my car. When he's done I can get my pills and head out on the highway before my enemies locate me.

"Sorry, I thought you were kidding." I add as he shakes his head with a coy smile.

"No worries. I bet you think a bar tender couldn't afford this car, huh?"

"Ha. Very funny Marcus, are you a want to be comedian too? You already stated you weren't really a bartender, but I've met some bartenders whose tips in one night are more than some people make in a week."

"Hmm, really?"

I nod.

"I guess I should change my profession then."

I giggle. "No doubt, maybe you should. Seriously, I love your car though. My favorite of all time in fact and if I could buy a new one, this is what I would choose. Mint condition from what I can tell."

"Yes, your reaction made that obvious. I'm glad you like it."

"More appropriately - love it! How long ago did you buy it?" I say too wired to stop myself and let the poor man get a word in edge wise. He's still smiling, I can tell he's proud of his car and likes I'm worshiping his vehicle.

"I'm kind of fond of it myself. I bought the car new several years ago." he murmurs gesturing me to get in. Wow, I can't remember the last time anyone's opened a door for me...if ever. I guess chivalry's not dead after all. My heart races and I am awkward as I scoot by him close enough to feel his heat. I'm holding my breath and time seems to stand still for a brief moment. Surprisingly he doesn't move back to give me more room as I slide down and into the seat, his eyes never leaving mine, yet I am so aware of every inch of his body.

"Thanks again," I whisper unsure of what I'm supposed to say at a time like this. My nerves ricochet from one spot to the next like a pin ball machine going crazy as I get into the car with a complete stranger. I mean... let's face it; I only met the man an hour ago. Yes he seems nice and bought me lunch, none the less I'm still barely acquainted with him. It's probably not very smart of me. Driving out on a deserted old highway with a man I met at a bar, and I don't possess any information about him accept he's on vacation.

He on the other hand holds plenty of facts on me. First my car is broken down on the out skirts of town and second I'm traveling alone. This could make things pretty easy on him if he was a rapist or killer. He could easily tell his friends at the bar he fixed my VW and I drove on safely. They would never discover the difference once he got rid of my vehicle in a nearby lake. Here I go again, honestly Issy, quit scaring yourself... everything is fine.

Getting into the driver's side of the Jag Marcus turns to me calmly speaking in his deep husky voice, "we need to take a quick detour by my cabin to pick up my tools and we'll be on our way."

My eyebrows shoot up in alarm and my right hand automatically reaches for the door handle. My body trembles, 'CABIN' -- Rings through my ears like symbols being slammed to each side.

Marcus glances at me sideways oddly then does the deep wonderful all out laugh again before saying, "woman, I'm not here to hurt you. My only intention tonight is to help a beautiful woman. If I wanted to seduce you, I assure you I could come up with a better plan than fixing your car." he leans closer towards me to wear our lips are almost touching and I inhale his sexy breath, "if my plan was seduction I'd do this." He licked his pointer finger and touched it to my lips giving me a serious heated stare while caressing my hand causing every nerve and muscle to dance,

"I could have easily hurt you when it was only you and I in the room, but I don't want to hurt you. You need to learn to trust people a little. Calm yourself, Issy."

I freeze. I swear my heart does somersaults around my chest as a full bodied blush takes me over shocked and appalled and at the same time wishing he would have done that with his lips while ecstatic at the same time He finally said my name, Issy. And my name never sounded so perfect. I let the joy of his lips uttering my name wash over me bathing in it for a brief moment, but my mind moves on and I wonder how whenever he speaks I automatically calm down? I swear the man hypnotized me with his voice, not to mention those eyes. I thought the room had only emptied in my head alone. This is weird... the room emptied in his head too. Did he actually make everyone disappear? What is he? I'm thinking he's magical. Not like me...something else altogether.

"What are you going on about? I'm fine. I was making sure the door handle was secure. I thought the handle felt wobbly like a screw was probably missing." I say quickly trying to cover up my foolish actions.

His eyes survey mine for a moment longer. Than he leans his head back again and lets out that incredibly sexy Santa laugh I've fallen in love with. "You worry too much Issy, were picking up my tools and driving to your car. I don't carry my tools with me obviously; look around limited space and all." He says grasping the wheel.

"Yes, of course like I said I'm fine with stopping by your cabin for tools," I say sticking to my story. Thinking duh, Issy you idiot. But I can't help it... and it's his fault. My brain seems to be mush and I can barely breath in such a closed off area with him...his scent is mouthwatering, almost appetizingly good tempting my palette. What would his flavor be like I wonder? Oh my God, did I really let my mind go there? I try to avoid his face. For some reason I refuse to think about Marcus Turns my insides inside out. Everything's a flutter. The man's a walking aphrodisiac. Still I can't control myself from taking a quick peek. His lips are perfect...Holy mother what I'd give to touch them. Simply reach my finger up to them following the outline of his flesh down to the fuller bottom lip and tug on down...,

We drive down the Highway a good thirty minutes in silence before he turns off on a much smaller road. An older dirt road and I start to worry yet again. Ax murderer comes to mind. We drive for another twenty minutes than cross a small old rickety bridge, he takes a sharp right turn between a cove of large pine trees causing me to fall towards him before I can right myself. His arm automatically goes towards me to protect me from falling even with my seat belt on. The contact from his touch lights a spark and we both inhale before we can hide it.

He clears his throat.

I turn my head away from him.

"Where you headed anyway?" he asks a few minutes later out of no-where surprising me. Marcus is not much of a talker something I admire in a man. Mainly because I'm not very good at small talk myself.

"Hmm?"

"You said you we're passing through."

"Oh. Umm, cross country."

"Where did you come from?"

"A long way from here,"

"Indeed." He says dryly, but to my relief doesn't ask any more questions.

A huge lake lies in the distance as we're reaching the top of the hill. Whoa, there is an enormous beautiful mansion size house directly in front of the lake. My breath catches. It reminds me of a Thomas Kincaid painting. This is almost too perfect, picturesque in fact. My mind questions why we're here though? I thought he said we were going to his cabin. I glance all about slightly confused looking for a cabin or at least another road leading to a cabin. The road stops here and this is the only place in sight.

"We're here."

"Where's your cabin?" I ask still looking around for a shack or at least a road leading to a cabin. "This isn't a cabin." I say pointing at mansion in question.

His lips curl up in a half grin, "What did you expect - a hole in the wall?"

"Well...yes, you said a cabin. Let me tell you something mister this," I point to Mansion, "Is not a cabin. A cabin is four walls with a flat roof on top and an outhouse out back!"

"Woman, this is to a cabin. A well-built cabin as a matter of fact. I should know I built it with my own two hands." He lifts both hands from the wheel making his point. His hands are large with long slim fingers, working man hands. Skilled hands, I guess if he built this beautiful mansion. Is there anything this man can't do? I bet he's done a lot of hard work with those two strong manly man hands. A shiver runs through the length of my body at the thought of what those two hands could do to me. I heat from the inside out. What is wrong with me? I can't seem to keep my mind out of the gutter when it comes to this man.

"Wow, seriously, I can't believe you built this?" I say thinking I stuck my foot in my mouth again.

"Why, you think I'm not capable?"

"No," I giggle out, "now you're putting words in my mouth I didn't say." If this man thinks this place is a cabin I'd like to see what he calls a house.

He chuckles. The garage door begins to slide open as he pulls up on the driveway, my heart starts beating rapidly. My right hand reaches for the door handle again as he pulls to a stop. I let out my breath I didn't realize I was holding in. He flashes his eyes at me questioningly and shakes his head back and forth slowly while taking a deep breath frustration obvious on his face. "You checking to make sure the door handle is secure again?"

"No, I was preparing to open the door - duh Marcus, why so paranoid."

His capable lushes' lips pucker, blue eyes dancing, "Uh huh, sure you were. You can come inside and get something to drink if you wish, while I change into my old working clothes and grab my tools. I'll only be a few minutes."

"It...It's ok I'll wait out here." I say crossing my arms in front of my chest.

"As you wish!" he gets out of the car looking amused and I'm pretty damn sure I detected him chuckling as he walked into the garage saying. "Ha. She calls me paranoid. That's like the pot calling the kettle black."

I sit here for a moment thinking about how foolish I probably appear to him before spotting the beautiful flower gardens and get out of the car to get a closer view. I can't believe he calls this place a cabin. More like a hidden paradise. Who'd of imagined such a wonderful place existed just over the hill. I am in love; seriously, I think in another life this would be my dream home. I could live here forever get married; raise a child or two... 'Ha, in your dreams' my inner-self admonishes bringing me back to reality before I sift too far away.

The supposed cabin appears new, but I can tell the structure is older just well kept. I wonder when he built the so called cabin. I would guess from the appearance alone he brought the building straight from Europe, but he states he erected the house himself. I guess he could have built the structure somewhere else and moved it here. This house is nothing like the rest of the homes in this area, though.

I gaze out over his gardens and am curious who does his gardening; Marcus called this place a vacation cabin. Does he think I was born yesterday? Anybody could tell this place is too well kept to be occupied only part time? Somebody puts a lot of love and attention into these gardens. These are not the easy kind of plants which naturally tend to themselves; no these are extravagant plants, flowers and bushes which take a lot of tending. They remind me so much of my mother and aunts gardens from my childhood, a memory from long ago. I try not to wallow in the past. This garden is different though with plants not native to here.

I walk around to the other side of the house where the lake is his front yard. Surprise a swimming pool. A little odd since its right in front of a huge lake but whom am I to judge. A hot tub sits hidden in the corner and I don't even want to imagine what's gone on in there. A thought of Marcus with other women darkens my mood for some reason I don't understand. So I continue my tour eyes widening at the size of his gigantic covered patio.

Not able to stop myself because of the magnificence of this place, I walk up on to his covered patio to take a better gander and at the same time to get out of what's left of the sun burning down on my head and shoulders. I fear if I don't get a blood pill soon I won't be able to handle the sun at all, But I can't do anything about my blood pill at the moment. Not until my car is fixed and I am able to find a doc to write me a script. Unless...? No I can't do it! I won't do it! He's been so nice to me I forbid myself to snoop! Unless it's my only option. I shake my head to scratch the thought.

Looking around all I can think is his furniture definitely didn't come from Costco, or Ikea or any of the other places with furniture for sale around here. This is custom made stuff like from France or Italy. Better than what most people can afford inside their homes let alone the outside. Now I wish I hadn't turned down the refreshments because I want to take a quick peek inside.

Potted plants and bushes surround the area with a small water fountain to the left side. I'm thinking the plants-like the furniture and house must be transplanted from Europe. They are breathtaking; again I wonder who does his gardening? His wife?

For some reason I can't explain I seriously hope he's not married and I didn't spy a ring on his ring finger. Nor did I view the Eternalmate sign of the heart shape imprint on his palm. But lots of men don't wear rings because of their work or other miscellaneous reasons. If he was my man I'd make him wear one to ward off single women out on the hunt. When he comes out I'll get a closer view at his left palm.

Weak not quite up to par, I sink down on one of his full cushioned comfy sofas and stretch my feet up on the matching ottoman. I drifted off for a few minutes, something I never do, because when I sense him and open my eyes he is standing before me with a couple of drinks in his hand grinning like the cat's meow.

"You went for a walk."

"Yes." I say quickly sitting up, "I simply couldn't help myself, your place was too alluring practically begging me to check it out."

"Thanks, you found my favorite spot," he adds looking out at the landscape causing my eyes to follow.

"No wonder, the views amazing." I say stretching my eyes out over the spectacular gardens with flowers of all colors of the spectrum, to the surprisingly clear deep blue lake beyond with Kokanee jumping from it I suppose, and the green foliage of the trees upon the Cascade Mountains swaying in the background.

"I thought you might like something cold to drink after all." He says bringing my eyes back to him.

I reach out and take it, what else could I do. I need all the blood I can get. He is tongue sticking out of my mouth drooling hot in his button fly Levi's and tight black Tee and my eyes wander over his wide shoulders and chest a little too long. Man oh man he's simply gorgeous. "Oh yes thank you I can't believe how hot it is today even in the shade." I say grasping on to the wine glass realizing I'm sweating again as I try to wipe the secretion off my forehead with my free hand, not really sure if it's only the sun getting me all heated up. I need to get back into the air conditioning and away from this man quick.

"You're welcome. Yes, it's unseasonably hot out here, and you shouldn't be out in it. I'll turn on the air." He pushes a button on the coffee table as he sits on the chair across from me and suddenly cool air rises up my legs coming from the floor and much to my surprise glass walls begin to move from all sides of the patio closing two sides of the patio off but not the one towards the front.

"Wow I've heard of heated floors, not cooled."

He grins raising both eyebrows, "sweet huh."

"Yep," I say with a sigh. "By the way who does your gardening...your wife?"

"No wife, Issy," he gives me a seductive approval-I'm pretty sure made me cream my panties as he comically lifts his left hand opening it so I could see his palm. "I do my own gardening. I enjoy working with my hands it comforts me." He adds mischief growing in those blue eyes. The same starry blue eyes I can't stop staring at to save my life.

My eyes widen. Did he say what I thought he said? How can something so innocent carry so many meanings? I blush. Holy cow my mouth went dry, heart rate sped up like a race car reaching the finish line of the Indy 500, breathing heavy, and I couldn't form a sentence if I had to. And all the while all I can think is number one' woo hoo -- He's not married.' Number two-he likes to work with his hands...Omg; the image his words put in my head sends me crooning. He clears his throat yet again reminding me he's waiting. "Oh, really?"

"Really, no wife Issy," he answers eyes sparkling. He stares at me and I get the sense he's trying to read me. I know he can't...we've never shared blood. Well, at least I think he can't.

"I meant, 'really,' you do your own gardening?"

His starry blue eyes turn into dark deep pools right before my eyes and I can't help but swoon. He is assessing me looking straight through to my soul! Smiling a cool smile he puts his hands over his heart and murmurs, "my apology Issy. I thought for a minute you might be interested in this poor mechanic -- bartender - carpenter, hell jacks of all trades.' You're breaking my heart woman." His sultry lips are playful causing me to want to suck on his full bottom lip. What is it with his lips - they're driving me nuts, doing weird things to my mind? They remind me of someone, but I can't quite remember who.

"Oh please." I say dryly but my heart swells at the sound of his words. How badly I wanted him to mean those words surprises me, but unfortunately his words probably means he's a player and therefore a smooth talker who is messing with me like every other woman he probably speaks too. I mean how could he not be? Look around girl...the man possesses everything and more! Why would he be interested in a low life like you? Check out the mirror...you're a mess! You're life sucks!

"What?" he asks doing the curly lip thing again the man is driving me nuts something about the way he curls them up completely- magnificently naughty. I wonder if he practices it.

"Oh don't try to play innocent with me there's probably dozens of women breaking down your door on a daily basis I don't need to be added to your list of admirers." Damn it! I should be kicked in the head. What a stupid thing to say to this man. I sounded like one of those 'brainless girls' throwing myself at him. Fishing for his attentions telling him I think he's incredibly hot when I did not mean to!

"Hmm, none I'm interested in. Seriously, you like my place?" he adds changing the subject; thank God, and I swear Marcus is most certainly aware of what he's doing to me.

"Who wouldn't?"

"Thanks, I'm glad you enjoy my work."

"Are you kidding I should be paying you for the privilege of gazing at them. They're breath taking. Did you transplant them or where did they come from?" I say in awe, and add before he could even think about answering, "I wish I could garden like this. Unlike you my thumb is black."

He chuckles, "Yes, I transported most of them from places all over the world. No worries about gardening you can be taught. Perhaps you only need to learn the fundamentals of gardening. Your thumb could be green too." He gazes at me curiously before adding, "I could teach you if you'd like - if you're planning to stick around town for a while longer?"

This time I clear my throat. His statement causes me to wonder if he would like me to stay around, but I don't say anything UN-sure if he was just being polite. He swallows the last of his beer before adding, "Well think about the lessons, the offer stays open for as long as you're around." he stands up. "Let's go fix your car?"

"Sure," I answer, fearing if I stayed even one more minute I'd never want to leave. What's wrong with me today? The choice is not mine. I can't stay here. The posse gets closer every moment.

"Ok, as soon as you finish your wine we'll head out."

The problem is as I finish my wine I realize I don't want to leave even though I must. The posse waits for no one. I long to venture inside his house to see what treasures lie within because If the furniture out here is any indication of what fills his rooms it must be spectacular.

"May I use your restroom first?"

"Well of course, but aren't you afraid I'll tie you up and try to take advantage of your gorgeous body, once we're inside." He says, blatantly checking me out, his eyes performing an all-out un-censored scanning of my form from my head to my tiny little pink toe. I gasp my mouth hanging open wide.

He chuckles. "You're pretty gullible aren't you?"

I blush.

He winks before walking over to the French doors and I'm happy to get a view of his manly backside and the way he moves is something to behold. Marcus is all muscle and masculinity radiating confidence. He opens the door with one hand and with the other does a swipe through the air while bowing gesturing me to come inside like a door man would do in 'Gone With The Wind' or some old movie..

"Now where did I put those hand cuffs?" his eyes search around the room.

My eyes widen briefly before realizing he's messing with me again. "Cute."

"Sorry, but you're so damn fun to tease." he sticks his elbow out for me to grab on to. "May I escort you my lady." Is this guy for real? He's so old school, but I like it.

I walk through the foyer and immediately stop! "Wow!" Marcus is freakin' rich? I glance all around me speechless. He turns his head towards me placing his index finger under my chin and presses up; closing my mouth I hadn't realized till that moment was open. I groan.

"Like what you see?"

"Uh Wow,"

He chuckles, takes my hand this time causing it to tingle and pulls me forward leading me to my throne. All I can wonder is can he sense the connection between us too? He didn't make any indication to show me he does so I'm wondering if I'm only affected by him and it's not mutual. The thought makes me sad for some reason even though I will be leaving soon either way. As soon as my car is fixed and I refill my Hemocil, which reminds me I need that pill. This basically leaves me with no choice but to do a terrible, un-thinkable low life thing like snoop through this, 'knight in shining armors' medicine cabinets. He leads me to the bathroom.

"Think you're able to find your way back to the living room?"

"Yes, I mean I'll admit this place is huge, but I'm pretty certain." I answer happy to be left alone a little while to wander this beautiful house. Hopefully I can find the master room and check out his medicine cabinet without being caught. Marcus gives me a skeptical gaze and I wonder once again if he can read me?

"Ok, well, rest assured I'll come and rescue you if it takes too long." he says walking away from me and I worry he figured out somethings up.

3

Snooping

Marcus

I hear her snooping through my room and most surprisingly my medicine cabinets. Why didn't she ask me for whatever it is she needs. I don't think she's a thief per say, but it's obvious she's looking for something specifically found in medicine cabinets. She doesn't appear to be an attic of any kind.

I wonder what her story is and more to the point why was she on one of the old highways in the first place instead of the freeway? When I asked her where she was from she had answered 'a long way from here' and hadn't answered the question at all. When I had asked where you headed, again she had avoided the question by saying 'cross country.' In my experience when someone is this vague they're running from something or someone.

So my next thought is whose she running from? She's terrified by whoever is hunting her to the point of shaking and always on edge. I'm curious if the aggressor is an old boyfriend or worse an abusive husband, but I didn't see an Eternalmate imprint on her left palm, when I turned and placed a kiss in the middle. Not a subtle way for me to find out if she had an Eternalmate, but I had to find out either way.

Her aroma calls to me and I want to understand her better. She's different in an alluring way. I can tell she's got a lot more going on in her pretty little head than she wants to admit. One things for certain though, she plans to keep on running as soon as her car is fixed. I'm not going to let her get away so easily. If she runs I'll go on a little road trip and see if I can rid her of her threat. I want more time with her to see where a courtship of some type might lead. She's mysterious. And cute with her whisky colored eyes and sweet little turned up nose. She's feisty - oh yeah the woman is my type, but at the same time I sense a little insecure. I can help her get over her insecurities if she'll let me. She's a Va'atacos, low on blood and I can tell she hasn't been to ground for a while, but my guess is not from choice.

Not a Suntanic by any means. Something else seems to be lurking inside of her and she seems extremely careful not to let whatever is inside her, come out. I can relate having a few secrets of my own, but I don't want to dwell on it now. I'm looking forward to learning all of the woman's secrets before I ever let her go, if I let her go at all.

She is coming my way. It will be interesting to see if she tells me the truth or if she lies. Her erratic heart beat tells me she's afraid her search took her too long.

"I was about to come looking for you. What happened, did you get lost?"

"Yes, sorry, but that's exactly what happened." She bats her eyelashes trying the sweet pursuit, "I couldn't help it. I was so busy admiring all your beautiful things I missed the left turn, and arrived at your amazing library instead." She states slowly, carefully putting the lie into words.

"My library?"

She nods wide eyed.

"I see."

"The pictures of majestic landscapes far from here, the furniture uniquely hand crafted out of specialty woods, the lamps made of crystal and gold, and even the books appear ancient. This entire house is like a museum." She continues blowing the hair out of her sensuous dark eyes. The woman is stunning in a way one would not normally think of as stunning.

I take her lie in letting her squirm a few minutes then shrug my shoulders while saying. "What can I say, I like old stuff. Did anything else keep you... besides my antics?" Her eyes blink and I can tell she's trying to keep them from betraying her.

"I didn't mean to insinuate you're ..."

"What?" I ask narrowing my eyes enjoying her cheeks turn slightly pink.

"Oh nothing."

Finally she drops down on one of my chairs taking a deep defeated breath grabbing a decorated pillow and placing it on her lap, hugging the thing to her chest like a child would do. She peers over at me defeated and says, "You possess superior hearing, don't you?"

I nod. "Yep, afraid so." She seems so vulnerable, but I can tell she holds strong inner strength not to mention the secret part of her she keeps well hidden, the part of her she is afraid to let out. I get the impression she suffers tremendously because of it, the same as I do.

"Terrific, can you read my mind too?"

"Yes...most of the time."

"What do you mean?" she asks nervously while she runs her fingers through her hair making me slightly jealous, because my fingers are itching to do the same thing. I can barely keep them at my sides. Her strawberry blond shiny hairs been tempting me from the moment I first laid eyes on her, when she first fell through the door at the Shitkick Bar glistening with sweat, crying out the words, 'Hallelujah." I heat at the memory.

My heart had stopped beating for a moment as I stared at the beauty. I actually couldn't move for a few minutes frozen in time as it were. She clung against the door breathing deep gulps of air as though she was starving for the coolness it would bring, her chest rising up and down, long toned legs spread slightly apart. She was stunning even dirty and covered with sweat and so weak and blood thirsty she had no idea that a room full of people were watching her every move.

Her heart beat pounding ever louder in my ear drums and her breathing speed up brings me back to her lovely face. Lovely yes even if she may be a thief, but I don't think so. My guess is she's running scared and out of options. I bet there's a good explanation for her snooping.

"I am a lot older than you for one which makes all my abilities stronger. How old are you by the way?" I add as an after though before thinking.

"Are you insane? Didn't you're mama tell you not to ask a woman her age?"

"Oh sorry, I was just curious." I say with a chuckle

"Well, in that case - not one day over a hundred and one," she retorts with a perky grin crossing her arms in front of her and I wonder if she's lying again. I believe most women tend to lie about things like age.

"So you're a young one - like I thought." Damn.

"Too young?"

"Not at all, but you on the other hand might think me a cradle robber."

"Oh is that so, well...please enlighten me."

"If you insist?"

"Oh, I do."

"I'm five C's." I say lifting my chin.

"Centuries...?" she retorts with a pretend cough while covering her mouth, "phew, you are old."

I'm shocked at her honesty. "Too old?" I ask with a thick tongue thinking, I could rock your world, baby. To prove my point I feel my heat seeking missile standup for the challenge.

"Not at all - perfect. I like my men older."

I grin. Happy to be informed, but it's something I need to think about a little more because as hot as she is we only met an hour ago. I'd like to learn all her secrets before I go any further. Not to mention the age difference. For some reason she seems so young. Not that I care about age, It's not a fact immortals worry about. I dispute her maturity, she appears in-experienced. No, she couldn't be. I'd bet money her sudden flirtations are an act she's trying to pull off to sway my thoughts from her snooping episode. Which I gather is exactly what she's up to.

For some reason I don't understand I want to reach out to her. Slip her within the folds of my arms for a long slow embrace to try and calm her over active heart. I'm actually afraid it's going to jump right out of her lovely chest. Which makes no since at all because I'm the one causing her reaction in the first place. This woman enchanted me somehow. Black magic under some kind of spell and I don't like it. Not one bit.

"Is that so?" I purr my words betraying me and unexpectedly I want more than anything to kiss her sweet full lips. Her whiskey colored eyes staring into mine is almost more than I can handle not to mention her lips so sweet, so full, and so perfect. One kiss and I might be able to forget all about them and get my mind back to deciphering a plan to stop these hunters. I focus my head by mentally shaking it, clear my throat and promptly change the subject before it goes too far. I don't want a woman. I'm the one who scoffs at my brothers for being in such a damn hurry to be locked up to a ball and chain around their neck. This flirting needs to stop now.

"Wouldn't you like to know?" her lighthearted grin spreads across her face enchanting me more.

"Yes, actually," I clear my throat, what am I saying and why can't I quit flirting with her? I must get back on track.

"Well let me ..." I don't let her finish the sentence.

"But for now let's get back to the subject at hand, shall we? To finish answering your earlier question age for one makes all of our senses stronger as you're aware, and I'm consistently controlled always honing my abilities keeping them sharp." Yeah right if only she could read my mind she would understand what a complete hypocrite I am. "My work as a Carpathian Devil..."

She groans.

"When not on vacation makes it imperative I keep them sharp at all times. Yes, Issy, I am a Carpathian Devil in my homeland, or as you would call me here a man of the law."

"Oh... you mean a police officer!" her eyes are big and round, a muscle jumps in her cheek.

I nod. "Don't worry Issy; I'm out of jurisdiction here." I chuckle because of the surprised facial expression like a little girl about to get in trouble from her father for something or other and I can imagine how cute she was with braids on each side of her face and pink rounded cheeks turned up, nose speckled with freckles.

"Umm I'm not worried. Why would I be worried there's nothing to hide?" She states nervously.

"I work with a lot of hardened criminals at the Carpathian prison Issy. I need to be able to read people and get in their heads to obtain any chance in hell at catching them, not to mention keeping them incarcerated."

"Well that's nice. You sound very accomplished at what you do Marcus. I bet your mama is very proud."

"I'm not sure if you meant that sarcastic or if you were being sincere, Issy, but yes I believe both my parents are proud of me. Why would I give them any reason not to be?"

"It must be nice to be able to say words like that with a clear conscience. Not very many people can."

"Issy, I realize you're just fishing for a fight to change the subject again, but I'll bite. I didn't say I've led a perfect life because I am a man of the law. I said I believe my parents are proud of me. Yes, there's been plenty of mistakes remember I'm five centuries. It wouldn't be possible to live this long without making any."

"I wasn't fishing...."

"The time for stalling is over. The answer is yes most of the time I can read you. Even if I can't read all of your thoughts all of the time, I can still read your body language like a book. With most people like you for instance, their body language tells more than their mind or mouth ever will."

"What do you mean like me?" she says clearly offended.

I stand up from the chair I was sitting on and slowly walk to where she is perched muscles tense yet feet positioned to run if needed. She's looking at me as if she's hanging on to every word. I lean over her chair putting my hands on the arm rests on each side of her and my legs straddling hers on the outside, barely touching her warm skin caging her in to show her I'm ready if she tries to run. Leaning towards her until our lips are only about an inch apart and her sweet breath fills my space clouding my head, "Now, let me rephrase the question, anything more you'd like to tell me before we drive to your car?"

She stares at me for a moment longer and I can see in the expansion of her pupils, she's fighting with herself trying to decide whether to confide in me or not. Her eyes clear decidedly and her chin sets firmly as she speaks. "No, but may I ask a question of you?"

"Ok - shoot?"

"First and most important are you Va'atacos?"

I'm speechless for a moment. Not exactly what I expected her to say knowing she was in my washroom five minutes ago going through my medicine cabinet. My Hemocil was in plain view. What game is she playing? I lean a few inches away from her a moment trying to read her. I can't help; but speculate where she's leading with this line of questioning. "Well, naturally. I thought you had gathered that already or you wouldn't be here with me tonight. On the other hand, perhaps you prefer to live on the edge. You want to dance with the devil, Issy?"

"No. I was almost positive not reading any bad vibes from you. And the reason I had faith enough in you to ride out here was because the owners Buck and Sophia at the bar seemed to like and trust you, but without coming straight out and asking...well, it's hard to be positive. Especially when you're an older vampire which as you stated is stronger and therefore better at hiding their true appearance."

I can't believe she used my words in her own self-defense against me.

I nod. She makes a good point.

"I need to ask you another question Marcus, now that you confirmed you're Va'atacos."

"I can hardly wait." She's right of course. I could easily be Suntanic and she would never sense the difference. So my thought is, good God is she crazy driving off to the middle of nowhere with a man she met in a bar?

"Okay, okay, calm down, I'm going to spit it out." She says grabbing a strand of hair that was hanging loose from the side of her face appearing nervous, "I'm out of blood pills and I don't possess a new prescription to be filled. I don't recall the last time I was able to go to ground for rejuvenation. The truth be told I wouldn't be surprised if there were a few warrants out for my arrest." She stops to swallow and brushes the braid behind her ear with a shaking hand. So she was looking for my Hemocil after all. "Marcus, at this point I'm literally a Suntanic waiting to happen."

"Why's that, Issy?" I ask surprised by the roughness of my own voice.

"I'm sorry I can't tell you my reasons. And my history shows you wouldn't believe me if I did."

"Try me."

"I wish I could, perhaps one day in the future."

"You mean if I earn your trust." Which I'm sure she doesn't expect to stay around long enough for me to do.

She glances down at her feet taking a deep breath.

"I realize asking you is against the law...and I hope you don't arrest me for this Marcus, but it's my only option. Could you lend me a couple of Hemocil until I can find a doctor later once my cars fixed, if my cars fixed, to write me a new script? The truth is I don't think I can go back out in the sunlight until I get one. So unless you want me as a lifetime house guest, well I mean..."

Her eyes widen mirroring mine after she made the ultimatum as she covers her mouth with her hands. She didn't mean to say those words if the red cheeks that followed are any indication. I stifle all the comebacks swimming through my head. I like the concept of her being my lifetime house guest when it's time for things like that. But for now all I can think is she's extremely lucky I'm not a Suntanic and didn't lure her out here for some other darker reason then retrieving my tools because at this rate she's too weak to fight.

More importantly she's desperate, which is never a good place to be in. Situations like this usually cause people to make huge mistakes, like snooping in someone's medicine cabinets who is trying to help you. The woman is obviously proud and not used to asking for anything. Even more important she came clean. Eventually I'll earn her trust and she'll confide in me with the truth. For now I'll help her and wait it out. What other choice do I have except to keep her as a love slave for eternity here in my house? I clear my throat before saying, "The offer is certainly appealing," *but I'd only want her willingly. I must do the right thing here.* "I could put you under protected custody for your own protection..."

She gasps.

"But how about instead I call my father..."

"Your father?"

"Yes, my father is part owner of the Pharmaceutical manufacturers."

"What...part owner?" If the wide eyes and the O shaped mouth are any indications - the woman is shocked. Yes we're filthy rich, but we don't care about those sorts of things. We've been around so long we've already had everything money could buy, and an important lesson you learn when you live forever is money matters naught compared to relations. My Eternalmate and children will come later when I'm ready.

Our father was detrimental in helping Nicholai invent the Hemocil, a guinea pig more or less. He was the man, who stood up and said, 'I'm your man,' when Nicholai needed a volunteer to be the first to try the elixir after our village had been slaughtered. The tests they put him through almost killed him a few times before the elixir was perfected so he deserves every penny he earns, but that's not why he volunteered. He did it to save us all from becoming like the monsters that had attacked our village.

"Yes Issy. Not a big deal. I'll call his assistant and she'll fax a script to the drug store. We'll pick the pills up on the way back to your car." I don't glance her way even though I'm tempted too. I understand she needs her pride to survive. "You ready to go?" I ask grabbing my car keys off the key hanger on the wall.

"Yes, I suppose we'd better. I umm, thank you."

About an hour later we've gone to town picked up her prescription and are now driving the direction of where her car broke down. We've driven several miles out of town and from the directions she's given were seconds away from where her VW broke down. As we get closer about two miles away we turn to each other knowing some force of danger is ahead. She says in a troubled tone, "my car is over the next hill, but I can tell something is wrong."

I nod, glancing her way for an instant and am surprised to see her skin turned a spooky white and her eyes appear hollow, "I can sense it too," I murmur.

"Quiet. Much too quiet!" I hit the brakes and do a one eighty in the middle of the two lane highway. One hand on the wheel and the other one automatically slide across Issy's chest holding her firm to keep her safe. All the while hoping whatever's out in the woods doesn't realize we're here yet. I'd like to understand what I'm up against first.

4

Witch Hunters

Marcus

"Any ideas on what's out there?" I ask her as we walk away from my Chevy Truck I chose to bring in case I need to tow her car, hoping she'll confide in me on her own. Wanting some facts on what we're up against and if we need back-up. What's got her so damn frightened? I mean, obviously by her actions alone she's hiding something momentous. Whatever is in those mountains is old and malevolent. Her eyes jump to mine wide and alert. I can tell she wants to tell the truth, but is afraid to trust me. Never the less this is obviously not only about her broken down car the woman needs a lot more help than she's claiming. She waits a beat too long before answering. Her eyelashes flutter closed so quickly most people would miss it, than as I expected - she lies.

"Nope, I don't think so."

"You don't think so, Issy? No idea at all?"

"Do you mean besides my car?"

I nod. "We both sense there's more going on out there then your car."

"Look all I can tell you for sure is my car broke down over that hill." She points to the hill in question, "That's it nothing more. Whatever else is going on in the woods has nothing to do with me." she says, turning and walking towards the hill. Hmm she can't even stare me in the eye as she lies to me. I guess I'll find out soon enough.

I shake my head and continue striding through the brush around the trees and into the beautiful scenery of the Cascade National forest. I can't worry about her lies now. Hopefully, soon I can prove myself and she will trust me enough to confide.

We decide to hike back to her car in the shadows of the trees to scope out what's going on. We could use our powers and fly, but since we both are on the Hemocil and therefore lost thirty percent of our powers. We choose to save them for whatever's ahead.

I don't worry about my powers because even with the thirty percent loss I can hold my own against any vampire.

My worry is for her. I'm not sure what kind of enemy we're up against and un- fortunately she won't say, although I can tell she's lying. I'm not sure how safe I can keep her and that is unacceptable to me. The one obvious point is whatever it is... it's not vampire.

I can tell by her vitals she is troubled and wants to forget about her car altogether and run. Not going to happen. Whatever is hunting her must be bad because simply put she's terrified. We've barely began to walk towards her car and she's already got a rapid heart rate and her pretty intelligent eyes are wide glancing all around her like an alley cat ready to pounce. She nee-dent worry anymore I'll do the worrying for her. I will be her sworn protector whether she likes it or not and I vow to keep her safe, one way or another.

We caught the scent of the wood and the wax burning and the sound of the crackle pop of the fire long before we saw the flames shooting up through the trees. The fire is no natural fire of wood and brush, oh no it's odor rubber and medal. The fire is burning out of control and it dawned on me. It's her car and more specifically her tires.

"We're getting close," she says covering her nose and mouth with the sleeve of her shirt looking like a jack rabbit ready to flee. "Ewe gross, what is that terrible stench?"

I don't say anything.

"Boy oh boy those flames are huge; do you think we should turn around?" She points toward the flames shooting above the trees.

"It's a wild fire, but I'm pretty sure it's contained." I confirm staring up at the fire lit night as we climb the last hill waiting for her to figure out what's burning herself. The rubber from her tires is what's making it so wild, but I don't want to be the bearer of bad news.

It only took a couple more seconds before she stopped in her tracks.

"Perhaps we should turn around now while we still can." Issy murmurs as her bottom lip wobbles, her face pales and her eyes fill with hollowness again. Haunted. No other words to describe her face.

I look hard at her for a minute. "If that's what you want? Why don't you go back to my truck?" I reach in my pocket for my keys. This man's never ran from a fight in his life and I'll be damned if I'm going to start now. But the thought of her being safe far from here is appealing to me, because if I need to kick some Suntanic ass - which I'm afraid, is what it's going to come down too. I'd rather do it without worry of anyone reaching her.

"No, it's not your fight. Come with me!"

"Who said anything about a fight, Issy? Are you expecting one?"

She glances a way.

"What's going on here? Any fool can tell you're hiding something. What are you so afraid of?" I ask taking a hold of her chin and lifting it up so there's no choice, but for her to look in my eyes when she answers.

"Noth..."

"I want the truth. Don't you understand I'm trying to help?

"I'm not sure."

"You're not sure or afraid to tell me? Which is it?"

She rolls her eyes down and murmurs so quietly I almost missed it, "I'm not positive, but it could be the hunters."

"Hunters, Issy?"

"Witch hunters..." she whispers trying to push my hand from her chin.

"Witch hunters, I wasn't aware there were any in these parts, but either way why would these supposed witch hunters be chasing you?"

"It's a long story I'll explain later when there's more time. We must get out of here now while we still can." She turns to walk away.

"Calm yourself," I say in my hypnotic voice to quiet and to command her. "Go to my car. Drive to my house. Go inside and wait there until I arrive. If I don't return within the next twenty-four hours, go to my room dig in my bottom dresser drawer under my jeans. There's a green note pad with a number on it. Call the number and leave this message only; Marcus requests your assistance." I say still in my hypnotic voice, "Can you do that Issy? Say you understand." She stands their gaping at me for a moment with a blank stare on her face, but her face changes as she comprehends. Let me tell you the woman is smokin-hot, when she is angry.

"Nice try." She hisses as her hands go to her hips. "Did you just try to hypnotize me Marcus?" she adds glaring at me.

"No...I mean, yes. It worked earlier."

"I knew it. Calm yourself Issy my ass, no wonder it sounded so soothing. The entire time you've been using voice control on me. The only reason you were able to get away with it earlier was because I needed blood. I had not taken a Hemocil or had blood for days. It's amazing what a few pints of blood sup will do and I'm much better now thank you very much and cannot be controlled so easily Marcus!" she spats as though it was a dirty word or something worse. Her hands on her much too thin hips - something I plan to resolve, silky hair like a whip flying in around her fuming face and I swear the ground shakes beneath us. Whiskey colored eyes now red wanting to blast me into nothingness and I'm almost afraid she could. Dynamite comes in small packages so they say.

Speaking of dynamite a thundering explosion below causes us to jump down to the ground. We flatten ourselves against the wild ferns and dirt crawling with our heads barely up high enough where we could see the valley below.

Issy gasps. I grab her head wrapping her to my chest muffling her cries.

"My...my car. My car's on fire. My home's on fire. How will I ever escape them this time?" Her body spasms and she fights the fear and anger rippling through her form. "If I do find a way to escape... what will I do? Where will I hide? They'll find me," - hic up, "they'll burn me alive just like my mother, my father, my coven."

"Shh...I'll never let that happen."

"You can't stop them - don't you see." She says eyes wide in alarm. "Nobody can stop them! They can't be killed." She cries out hysterical struggling to pull away from me, to run. "They're the undead. And they will stop at nothing to kill me!"

"Well, I hate to state the obvious, but so are we." I remind her quietly holding her in place, surprised with her strength. "What's so different about them? Why are they hunting you?"

"No. They're not like us - don't you understand. They're immortal witch hunters. Don't you dare eye me like I'm insane and belong in a mental ward. You don't need to tell me the facts sound crazy. Why do you think I never share this with anyone? I learned a long time ago nobody will believe me. This is the reason I couldn't confide in you. I'm sorry I inadvertently involved you at all. I thought they were farther behind me and I had more time." She sniffles, wrapping a piece of her hair around her ear, looking around searching for the quickest way to escape, I presume.

I sense movement over the hill and turn my head back to the scene below. The fire lessened in its severity and seems to be burning out, at least where the car is concerned. Five giant sized men with hideous scents even from this range. I can tell she's right. They're not Vampires. What they are exactly I couldn't be sure, but if I had to guess it could be zombies dressed as witch hunters. Impossible.

Their clothes are old school reminding me of the witch hunter's era around the sixteen hundreds. I'm talking centuries ago. Wide black brimmed hats upon their heads. Chains around their necks - it is said they protect from the witches spells. Covering their shoulders and bodies are large black cloaks. Somber clothing like what the Templars of Sigma would be wearing. Stuck in their clothing, I can bet are weapons of all types, anything to use to torture or kill a witch, garlic, knives etc., around their wrists they wear the sign of their membership to the order, a symbol of the twin - tailed comet.

Skin hangs loosely from their face, neck and hands proving the hunters should not still be around anymore than we should. Zombie or getting with modern times Walker, comes to mind. The problem is I'm not quite sure if they are actually dead, or alive? On the other hand I'm not getting a heartbeat from any of them. Their eyes are trance like black and cold as death and I can tell immediately their under an old spell

In the meantime what interests me the most at the moment is what the witch hunters are building. All five hunters are standing by cross like stakes pounded deep into the earth and reaching forty feet into the air. The stake in the middle reaching another five feet into the air could be Issy's twin nailed to it, which startles me at first. In fact oddly enough all five stakes hold some sort of porcelain like handmade dolls nailed to them. Painted faces, with what appears to be real hair of silk attached, reminding me of effigies. Below the stakes, each of the five is building huge bon fires.

Issy pushes at my chest as they light the stakes on fire, using torches that seemed to appear out of nowhere. Trying to see what's happening below Issy takes one gander, stiffens, cries out, "Mama," and promptly passes out cold. Ahh Shit!

All I can surmise from what Issy said the doll looking so much like her is to signify her mother. Could be the others are symbols of other family members or other coven members as she accidentally called them earlier. Either way it's a sign they're here. They're coming for her and we need to get the hell out of here.

5

New Beginning

Issy

My eyes snap open and I am startled immediately having no idea of where I'm at. I sit straight up in bed looking all around me ready for any sign of danger slipping into my fighting stance ready to attack if need be. The last thing I remember is being in the woods with Marcus. How the hell did I get here? Wait... Marcus, bed. I glance around this room and see the old world decorating of Italy; then it dawns on me. This must be a guest room at Marcus house. How did I get here? I fall back onto the bed, confused. The feather bed is so soft. I don't recall the last time I was able to sleep in a bed and not my old station VW wagon.

I glance down experiencing the unfamiliar softness of the silk as it slides against my tender skin. Wha ...what the hell? I jump up to my knees looking down at myself. Never as in ever has my skin worn something this skimpy or this soft. Silk...I'm wearing silk. Sleeping in silk sheets to boot, I realize as my knees begin to slide apart. I think it must be a miracle or I must be dreaming because this can't be right. How did I get into this nighty?

I detect something else, my hair is wet. I comb my fingers through it trying to remember something, anything. It's as though I was sweating, but my clothes are dry and besides this room is chillingly cool, so the air-conditioning works real fine in here. So why is my hair wet?

I slowly lift my feet over the side of the bed and drag my body the rest of the way out of his bed looking around for my clothes and boots. They are nowhere to be found. I walk into the bathroom scratching my head wondering if perchance I was still so out of it from lack of enough blood and rest I actually showered and its skipped my memory. So it's possible my clothes are hanging from the stall. Wow, I let out a low whistle, so this is how the rich live. Two toilets and two sinks odd if you ask me I mean what's the point? The money could be given to the poor.

When I finish walking through the threshold the first thing I note no clothes laying anywhere near the shower or the huge hot tub bath. The second is me full bodied in the mirror. I stop in my tracks. I stare mesmerized. When did I grow up to appear like this? I wonder confused, funny I never noticed the resemblance before. If my mother wasn't dead I would think she was standing in front of me. I could be her twin. I must be close to her age now, but I'm not sure. Peering at me like this snaps back my memory of last night. Mama! Oh God the wooden cross stakes. The bigger one in the middle with the long blond silky hair and face was too close of a resemblance to my mother, to me. I think it was a warning symbolizing my mother's death. They're sending a message. They want to remind me painfully how they killed her and all the rest of my coven, as my mother would say.

I am the last living member as far as I'm aware. I think they plan to take their time killing me slowly, causing me to suffer any way they can. The hunters called us witches, but my mother told me we were not. The problem is I think she lied to protect me at the time. I was still a child she probably feared I would say or do something in front of the wrong people, giving us away. It was such a bad time for witches.

The power that lies within me I fear if ever unleashed would be un-controllable. I won't let that happen. A few slips through the years put a deep fear in me. The only time it's happened is when someone pinned me in a situation where I am under pressure or threatened. I never call for the power. I'm not even sure how and I don't want to figure it out. It scares the crap out of me.

I hear a slight knock at the door and walk back into the bedroom as Marcus walks in carrying a tray. He is startled as he stares at me his eyes slowly perusing my flesh from head to tiny little toe, licking up every curve and cove. Leaving me with small tingly currents singing throughout my body doing strange things to my insides. I don't recall anyone inspecting me like this before and believe me it's not something I'd forget. It's full of heat almost scorching me from afar. He's worshiping me with his eyes. Skin heating to a warm glow of early winters fire and I can barely breathe. I stand here like a melting pot enjoying his sensuous approval.

When he finally reaches my eyes again I am wringing wet. Unable to move or even do the respectable thing like grab a blanket, or cross my arms over my body anything to cover myself from him. I'm in awe soaking Marcus in the same way as he had leisurely taken me in. Marcus clears his throat not looking away and the energy dancing between us is almost more than I can bear. Then when I think I am unable to pull away from this spell he opens his delicious mouth and speaks.

"Sorry, I thought you might be hungry," he falters for a moment before continuing, his voice husky, starlight eyes capturing my heart and squeezing, "so I brought you some nourishment. How are you this morning?" my eyes are still drawn to his delicious lips and can barely comprehend his words. I'm floating outside of my body now my stomach swirling round and a round.

I put one foot in front of the other stepping towards him without another thought. My heart is thumping like a herd of wild stallions running through an open field. He is so stunningly handsome and even more so unbelievably kind. A man like him should be savored and adored. He helped me, without me even asking him to. More than once, this is the first time a man offered to help me since my father was alive, without wanting something in exchange. He on the other hand asked for nothing in exchange. There's something about Marcus that makes me feel safe and at the moment coveted. He's exactly the kind of man my mamma told me to wait for. I want to be with this man. It's time to make a stand.

He takes a step towards me our eyes tuned straight to the others. I melt slowly like molten lava sinking into the floor beneath my feet. He stops apparently seeing the raw emotions in my face. His eyes are hungry in a way my eyes never witnessed hunger before and it's evident he wants to devour me, and joy fills me as I realize for the first time in my life I want this man more than anything to consume me, and I want to do the same to him every single adorable ounce of him.

"Issy." He says in a deep, low, questioning tone sitting the tray on the dresser. "Are you alright?" his voice deepens even more to a gravely purr, lips lifting into his sultry curl I can't deny. My feet are running towards this man before my mind even has a chance in hell of preventing me. I jump into his arms as he catches me scooping me in the air legs wrapping around his long waist his hands on my butt. Lips to lips and his meaty flesh is sizzling like a fire drawing me into the wicked hot flame, sucking me in like a tornado heated and moist like I knew they would be.

A fever grows within me juggling my insides I am so consumed by him. A torch so hot I fear it will burn us alive, but I can't stop. This man can kiss like nobody's business and I fear if he ever takes his lips from mine I will be useless forever more. They are soft smooth yummy lips, thick full tantalizing lips, demanding won't take anything less than what I can give lips, teasing me pleasing me lips, scandalous lips, oh they are ravishing, urgent lips, slick, juicy, smoldering steamy, brandy tasting, succulent lips. My head is spinning; my clothes are falling to the floor.

Holy shit - we fall to the bed rolling, stripping off each other's clothes like we can't wait another minute to be naked together skin bare and slickened with sweat. We're biting and pinching, moaning and groaning, grabbing, licking ooh the licking, smelling, caressing, circling every part of each other's skin again and again. When he takes my right breast into his mouth I almost melt from the heat. As he bites down I scream out from the pain, it hurts it hurts so damn good. My head is spinning; my body is craving wanting all of him. I can't seem to get enough "...please... please Marcus."

"Please what? Issy...say it. Tell me what you want. Anything at all just say the words."

"I I ..."

"I -- what?"

"I don't know."

"Issy. I think you do." He purrs in my right ear before he scrapes his teeth lightly across my lobe causing me to shutter.

"I want everything. I want it all. I want you."

"Show me Issy; show me where you want me." He reaches out his hand and places it around mine. "Do it now... take me where you want me to be."

Oh my God do I place his hand where I want him...need him...do I dare? I start to slowly move our entwined fingers down over my belly towards the place at the most secret part of my junction that at this moment is uncontrollably driving me crazy. More like insane. It wants to be touched and it demands to be filled with an urgency way beyond the both of us. My nerves are all over the place. Such an uncontrollable need fills me and it's a bit scary. More like overwhelming. Talk about a force of nature. I accept without a doubt I would do almost anything to fulfill this undeniable craving between my legs.

"Ahh so this is what you want..." he cups my sex and lightly rubs, I moan and my hips begin to move towards his hand and there is nothing I could do to prevent it, but this need grows stronger by the minute with each skillful touch of Marcus hands and the more he rubs the more I need oh so much more. My lower muscles are clenching a suction so strong begging for something, "Please." I hear my voice beg...

"Please what, Esmeralda?" he uses my birth name his words so low, so dark, so dangerously sexy, reverberating through every cell ending of my body egging them on and bringing them to life.

"Please more..." I breathe barely able to speak.

"Oh you want more huh? Is this what you want, Issy?" his thumb moves to my nub and I cry out from the explicit sensitivity there. "Umm, you like this don't you baby. You want more of this don't you?"

"Yes, yes please Marcus." He chuckles low and deep. "Here you go baby I'm going to take real good care of you..." he slips his index finger in between the folds and finds my wetness and I almost freak out from the surprise of it all because there are no other words to explain it, but freaking amazing, my hips are reaching for more while my lips are praising, "Oh yeah, oh baby... you're so damn good." My head rolls back and my eyes close as he continues his penetration and I lose my mind for a while.

"Well if you like that you're going to love this Issy." He says after I come back down to earth. Then he slips his finger out of my most private parts and I cry out, "No,"

He chuckles. "Shh - wait for it," he slides down my body licking, sniffing, and kissing as he goes and the next thing I come in contact with is his tongue gliding over my most sensitive core and I almost jump out of my skin. I whimper calling out his name, "Marcus, oh sweet..." them it happens something so fierce I could never explain it as it takes me over mind soul and body and I am now in outer space catapulting through the sky in complete cosmic skyrocketing bliss. I am laughing and crying at the same time it's so damn good and he doesn't stop he continues lapping me up and so do I rocketing further and further from my mind until I think I can take no more. He stops and slowly moves back up my body kissing, licking, sniffing and caressing, he nuzzles my neck and his manly parts nudge against my inner thigh bringing me back from my delectable high because he is huge. I moan.

"Are you ready, are you sure you want this Issy? It's your last chance to back out I won't be able to control myself once we begin."

"Yes, can't you tell how much I want you?" He kisses me again with so much heat I catch on fire we kiss and we roll around on the bed going at each other as if we are not able to get enough of the other, never wanting this to end. I can't describe what came over me, but whatever it was I can't make myself stop. I need this man inside of me and I want to please him in return.

Round and round we go consuming each other to the point there is no longer two of us. We are so entwined as one, our fingers and tongues lapping each other up enjoying the hell out of one another. Finally as I think I couldn't reach any higher he turns me over bringing his hands to my hip lifting my hips to where I'm on my hands and knees and he's behind me, "You're so wet baby you're so ready for me," he grabs a hold of my hips and in one smooth hot searing move he slams his vessel all the way inside of me. I'm afraid I might burst as tears of pain and joy fills my eyes, he pushes a little farther than when he is completely buried inside me he stops and both of our breathing is ragged when he reaches for my head and turns my face back towards his. Shocked blue eyes to tear glistened brown.

"Why...why didn't you tell me Issy? Did I hurt you?" He whispers gritting his teeth and I'm afraid he is furious, but I don't care.

"What," I try for coy ignoring his question all together as though it's no big deal even though it's a huge deal, a life changing deal, but he doesn't need to discover that right now. I lick my lips as my hips start to slowly move towards him wanting, needing, and searching for something I can't describe. The movement of my muscles around him causes his manhood to grow stronger larger inside of me and I am amazed at how big he is. My own body seems to adjust perfectly with his. The pain was nothing like I had overheard it should be as he broke through my virginity and what was left of my childhood, and made me his woman.

"Issy, you'll be the death of me," he purrs as he lifts me higher to a place I could not imagined possible, without being there to experience it for myself. I am changed forever.

As I awake I reach for him wondering why his arms are not tightly around my waist like they were every other time I was revived from him this day. His side of the bed is cold; my fingers only finding silk sheets.

I open my eyes knowing I am alone. I sit straight up in bed stiff like a zombie from a horror movie because I am sore all over. I throw the covers away from my body pulling my legs to the soft Persian rugged floor. I stand up noticing I am fully naked and a shiver runs through me remembering as to why. Oh yeah. I smile recalling how fast the green silk teddy he had dressed me in had disappeared. How he had taken me savagely at first, but the next time so sweet and lovingly as though I was a different woman with whom he had started with.

Next I go in search of my clothes once again as I did earlier today only to find they're still nowhere to be seen. All I can presume is they were ruined last night. If that's the case I worry what I'm going to where? Or he's washing them for me. I giggle out loud picturing Marcus doing laundry. He did say he likes to work with his hands I smile at the thought remembering what he did to me with those hands earlier. And it is so sweet to be a woman at last.

In the meantime what's a girl to do? I walk into the bathroom once again spotting his big marbled and so appealing hot tub bath and decide finding Marcus can wait a few minutes more. Besides after further review I sense him scurrying around cooking down below and the aroma is mouthwatering so I'm no longer too worried about his whereabouts. I can't even recall the last time I was able to take a bath besides sit in a hot tub. I'm safe here especially with Marcus strong holds on the property. He states their unbreakable and since he's a Carpathian devil I believe him, and am going to try to enjoy this break for as long as possible.

A half an hour later I walk down stairs slowly somewhat embarrassed which is odd after what all we did in almost every room on his second floor, wearing his robe I found hanging on the washroom hook.

He spies me immediately as I peak around the corner. His mouth crooked up in a grin. "I was beginning to wonder if you were going to sleep all day." He teases and I turn to putty in his hands thinking of all the ways those lips touched me earlier. I flush.

"I borrowed your robe," I say stating the obvious a bag of nerves. Not exactly sure of what to say to a person … I mean a man, shit…this gets worse, a man I only met yesterday. I'm scandalous dressed in red wrapping my hair behind my ears trying to glance everywhere except back at him.

"I can see that," he says with an arched brow eyes looking right through me and I swear into my soul. "Are you hungry?" He asks, pulling out a chair for me. Once again proving chivalry is not dead. I sit.

"A cook too, is there anything you can't do?"

He chuckles shaking his head, "Not once I put my mind to it."

"It smells delicious what is it?" I say my mouth watering from the wonderful aroma.

"To tell the truth I don't recall the official name, hmm, let me think bacon, potato, egg, onion, cheese - skillet fry?" he answers with a furrowed brow.

I chuckle, "sounds good to me. I don't recall the last time I had a home cooked meal. It's been..." I set my pointer finger to my temple trying to remember the last time, but alas it's been too long so I simply say, "forever."

He nods as his eyes flash toward mine with something I can only interpret as pity and it ticks me off for some reason.

"Where are my clothes and boots?"

His lips turn up playfully and it dawns on me where I saw those lips before, oh my God, 'Elvis lips - Marcus lips are Elvis lips, sexy beautiful naughty curled Elvis lips,' I think as he says, "What's the hurry? I kind of like what you're wearing now. My robes never looked better." His voice deepens his eyes sparkle and I get the impression he thinks I'm his present on Christmas morning and he can't wait to open me up. I imagine Elvis Pressley looking into the eyes of Ann Margret singing Love Me Tender and am mesmerized for a moment. I want him again. I cast my eyes away as I seem to heat from the inside out spreading across my limbs, afraid he can read what I'm thinking as my palms begin to sweat. Just breathe.

"All the same I need to get dressed sometime," I finally whisper.

"Hmm, If you say so." he saunters out of the room into a side room off the kitchen I can only assume is some sort of pantry or laundry room. On his return he is carrying my clothes washed and hung on hangers, boots polished cleaner than they were when I bought them at the Goodwill three years ago.

This time I blush. "You shined my boots?"

"Eat Issy." was his only response. His playful eyes now serious as he once again clears his throat signaling me my words made him uncomfortable. I hope I didn't insult him again is my only thought as I take a bite of his mouth watering bacon potato creation. "Mm...YUMMY."

He hadn't tried to kiss me or mention anything about last night or what we had done today. I was deeply grateful not willing to dig into those feelings quite yet. So we ate in quiet awareness both of us with too many things on our minds and too many questions about each other's lives.

After we finished eating and the dishes were all done and put away Marcus says in his sweet dark hum catching me off guard, "We need to talk about some things, but it will need to wait. Get dressed, companies coming."

6

The Clan

Marcus

I walk away from Issy with a wobbly awkwardness. The woman makes me comfortable in her presence yet at the same time like a teenager going through puberty. I'm not familiar with the oddness of all these new emotions. Being inside her sweet body today did something monumental to me, and I am forever a changed man. Thinking back I'm not exactly sure of how everything occurred, it's all a sweet blur.

One minute I had knocked on the guestroom door forewarning her I was entering. The next moment she was standing before me in the sexy hunter green teddy I had bought in town yesterday, as we waited for her Hemocil prescription to be filled. The minute I had seen the silky piece of fabric hanging in the window, I swore one day I would enjoy nothing more than to see her wearing the gown. Never in my wildest erotic dreams did I expect for it to happen this soon and even more surprising was how quick it landed on the floor. I smile at the thought thinking the Gods must be pleased with me to give such a precious gift.

I'm not sure if it's because of the wolverine or the man, but her scent had literally driven me crazy. There was no way around it I had to sniff, than lick every single inch of her body and claim her as mine like the beast demanded, doggie style. I can only hope she was too lost in her high from the orgasms to discover what I was doing. At one point I was a little afraid I wouldn't be able to control the beast, but my hormones took over and I was a gone man.

My mood darkens at the thought. Who am I kidding; I don't see how I can let her go now. The thought of another man touching what's mine makes me sick to my stomach and blind with rage. Mine. Shit!

Aware she was. I could never imagine how well her body would respond to mine. Virgin. What an unexpected surprise. How on earth did this goddess keep the men at bay? And a more appropriate question is why she saved herself all this time to give it away to me so freely? We met yesterday for crying out loud.

I'm not complaining, but it brings some severe thinking to the table. Problems I'm going to need to deal with. Issy took my choice away by not telling me before we had sex. Not right. Not right at all. Now I get to live with regret of touching her so savagely. It's supposed to be sweet and gentle the first time. I can never rewind this in her memory and it makes me angry, my hands fist wanting to hit something in retaliation. But the way she came at me was like a woman who had no qualms about what she wanted and her prize was in sight, as though she had sampled it before.

My mind returns to Issy when I acknowledge her exclaim behind me, "Company...what company? You said we were safe!" A sting of guilt runs through me when I sense the panic in her voice; as her footsteps fall in behind me walking up the stairs.

I stop and turn to talk to her midway wanting to assure her there was no danger unless you call my rowdy ass brothers danger, but before I can explain I am stopped in my tracks. I fight for control.

Holy Shit this woman is one smoking hot lady. She is hastily throwing her clothes on behind me. I groan as she covers her high full breasts with a tank top wanting to pull it back up over her chest and put my lips to her rose buds suckling like a new born babe, and when she pulls those miniature sized little blue jeans up and over her slightly on the thin side rounded hips, I want to scoot them right back down inch by

slow inch licking and sniffing. The woman wears no under clothes probably because a lack of funds, but either way it makes her body even more
enticing.

Wow! I stare at her – even underweight the woman is too hot for her
own damn good. If there was a little more time I'd lay her down right
here and now making love to her on the steps. Unfortunately my clan is a
loud bunch and I got wind of them entering the backside of my property
a few minutes ago. Damn! I clear my throat and shake off the lust I'm
experiencing for her right now as best I can.

"It's ok Issy, nothing to worry about. It's only my clan."

"Your clan?" she retorts with anger in her eyes.

"Yes, I sent for them last night."

"Oh no. Marcus – why'd you call them? I don't want any other innocent's involved. It's bad enough I brought you into this mess. I need to
leave pronto before they get here."

"Like I'd let you..."

"Let?" she lifts her chin in defiance giving me a sizzling glare.

"Yes. And it's too late either way. They're here. This is what we do. We
hunt the bad guys Issy!"

"But..."

"No but's, stay in here tell I come and get you."

"You're awfully bossy this morning." She retorts whiskey eyes narrowing hands slipping to her hips.

I grin, and give her a quick kiss on the tip of her nose as we reach my
bedroom tenderly backing her in wanting to shield her from their presence until I explain what's happening with the witch hunters, and proper
introductions are met.

"M-a-r-c-u-s," Maximus antagonized voice bellow at the top of his
lungs. Great – my clans here and they don't sound real happy about it. I
can't blame them considering it's only been a few years since we banished
Crucia to the Carpathian Prison. We've all been trying to get are lives
back together after what was a five century long ordeal in which I don't
want to wallow in right now, but It is the exact reason I'm here so far away
from all of them on an extended vacation in the first place.

I needed a break from everybody and everything. Free time for once in my entire life is what I craved. Too damn bad the reprieve didn't last long! Even though, I'll admit I'm looking forward to the pleasure of their company after being together most of the time for the last five centuries it gets a little lonely sometimes without them, a fact they will never get wind of.

Get a drink and I'll be down in a minute. I group message on our blood only line as I head back down the stairs and into my study to grab my brandy. Secretly hoping Issy will stay in my room like instructed. At least until I can explain what she shared with me this afternoon about her past and the witch hunters before she had finally passed out from pure exhaustion that is, after we had spent hours of hot and heavy sexual activities. I smile, looking forward to many more nights with her.

"Hello brothers," I say stepping into my greeting foyer somewhat upset to see their women had come too. I had picked up their voices miles back, but what could I do about it at this point in time. Send them packing with suitcases in their hands. It would serve my brothers right and I would try it, but my brothers would pack there few things and leave too and I need them. Raising my eyebrows I amended, "Ladies I'm happy to see you." I lie embracing my brothers one by one with a slap to the back in true man style.

Luckily my poker face rocks because the last thing we need here right now is more 'women' to worry about I think irritably. What were they thinking, I send for their help tell them the world might end, ok I exaggerated a tad bit, but still they bring their wives along to help?

I cast a scolding glare at my brothers to show I'm not pleased and say, "Men, grab your drinks and follow me." As we walk to my larger study slash library because there are more chairs, I relent and call back over my shoulder, "ladies make yourselves at home, you're assigned the same rooms as when you visited last year and there's plenty of food and drinks in the kitchen.

It's not that I'm not happy to see them. I need them safe and I need my brothers to be able to concentrate on the problem at hand and not worrying about their women.

I ignore Maximus groan. He's still uncomfortable with leaving Carrabella's side. Which is to be expected, I mean good God I don't understand how he handled it at all. I couldn't imagine my own Eternalmate disappearing on me over and over again no matter how many safeguards I had on her, let alone it continuing to happen for five centuries with the added bonus of her having amnesia each time. It crushed me to keep Maximus from killing Crucia for what he had done. But I'm a man of the law and every-man gets a trial whether they deserve one is not the issue.

Truth be told I wanted to kill Crucia too. We all wanted to kill him. Crucia single handedly had destroyed all of our lives for four centuries. My blood boils at the memory. Maximus doesn't need to worry though, I check on Crucia often. He will never escape his hell; Big brother made sure of it. Only time will heal what's been done to them, and luckily there is plenty...a whole eternity to be exact. It's taken its toll on all of us though. I scratch my two day shadow reminding me I need to shave before touching Issy again, I lift my eyes to the ceiling curious of what she's doing up there. Hoping she will stay in the room like I told her to.

Treyvon snaps me out of my reverie by asking, "So who's the blond upstairs in your room brother and what's so damn important you drug us back to Washington?"

"Stay the hell away from her." Shit, I had forgotten about what flirts my brothers are.

"Whoa!" Treyvon laughs, hands palms out in the air. "Don't look at me my woman's upstairs unpacking. You'd be better off to warn them." He uses his thumb to point back at our two younger brothers, James, and Anthony, standing behind him. They both laugh. Again I inwardly groan.

"There's a woman upstairs?" James asks looking surprised and pointing his head towards the stairs.

"Let's go find out." jokes Anthony bumping elbows with James starting towards the stairs. Clowns, as if they think I would allow them to take even one step.

I grab them both by the shoulders before they could take another step and lead them back into the study pushing them both down into my deep leather chairs. "You idiots don't even think about it unless you want to deal with me. She's under my protection - so hands off!"

They scoff for a moment, but realize how serious I am and back off. We talk for a while having a couple drinks together and catching up on the rest of our clan. Afterwards I explain to them all the facts about the five witch hunters.

I described to them all the details she enlightened me with. "Issy's father was vampire, but her mother was more than likely a witch and burned at the stake. However Issy pointed out her mother and Aunt Callie denied being witches. Issy thinks they withheld the truth from her because of her youth, and they died before she was old enough for them to tell her the truth of what they were. Issy witnessed the death of her mother Lily, as a child while hidden in the trees. Her mother with her last few breaths had screamed in Issy's mind to run and never stop running, directly before she had destroyed her once best friend a Demigod by the name of Meredith. Blown her into smithereens from what she said."

"Wow, if she does that to a friend I'd hate to see what she does to her enemies." says Maximus in a dry tone.

"No shit." agrees Treyvon.

"Now wait a minute guys, she had her reasons."

"What reasons, did a man come between them?" asks Anthony.

"Yes, and no. Meredith had brain washed the witch hunters with her gift of persuasion, and used them to trap and kill Jonathan, Issy's father."

"Vengeance, damn good reason." says Maximus.

"Yep the Demigod deserved what she got. So after Lily destroyed Meredith, in a fit of rage she had cast a spell on the witch hunters, bounding them to walk on the earth for eternity or until all evil was gone."

"What? Impossible." says James.

Maximus, Treyvon and Anthony stare at me with their mouths hanging open shaking their heads in agreement.

"What he said," says Anthony pointing at James.

"Exactly, and here's the funny part; they were to only do good will to all they come across for as long as evil existed."

"Bullshit! Now you're pulling our legs." Maximus exclaims.

"Nope, true story."

"So as you can imagine the problem is she didn't explain to them her idea of 'evil' or 'good will,' before bursting into flames herself."

"So that means what exactly?" asks Anthony.

"Well I think the answer is kind of obvious when you think about it. Their idea of 'doing good will' and or 'evil," I use quote signs, "was already stained on their brains by Meredith whom Lily had destroyed."

"So she out smarted herself and instead of helping her daughter she doomed her." says Treyvon.

"Yes, basically. There was no way to change their minds after both women were deceased. So the moral of the story is they believe they must kill all witches and any other super natural characters they come across, not caring who they trample in-between."

"Why should we believe this woman, Blondie?" Treyvon asks, voice full of sarcasm, eyes dancing knowingly.

"Issy," I bark testily. Wondering how he knew she was a blond in the first damn place. I casually glance towards the stairs. Not there. I wonder if she peeked out the window as they were coming in.

"Seems a little far-fetched to me," agrees Anthony, "I don't understand how they existed the last hundred years without us knowing hide nor hair about them. On the other hand you didn't send for us without some kind of proof." One of his dark eyebrows is lifted waiting for confirmation. Anthony's eyes so much like Maximus you would think he was Maximus's twin instead of Treyvon.

I nod.

Maximus stands up and heads for the bar as though he's not paying attention, but I comprehend he's mulling things over waiting to get all sides before committing either way. He makes a drink and listens.

"Marcus, why do you trust this woman - Issy?" James asks slowly knowingly as though he's seeing it for himself and I worry he is. Sometimes it's really irritating to be aware he can see things not intended for his eyes.

He was granted this power as a seer during the change centuries ago when we were still children.

The problem is he wasn't granted the choice of when or how to use it. He can't summons the power or refuse it. The visions come to him on their own whether he wants them or not. The slight grin on his face so slight I almost missed it leads me to believe he saw more than I'd like.

Damn! I start to answer them when Maximus murmurs so quietly it was almost a whisper. "He's seen them." My eyes fly to his, "Am I right?"

I nod. "Well of course. Do you think I'd waste your time otherwise?"

7

The Witch

Before anything else can be said we overhear screams coming from upstairs sounding as if their coming from both Carrabella and Brenn simultaneously and all I can think is, Issy. My brothers and I all appear at the top of the flight of steps within moments. The other men ready to kill to protect their women.

Issy is standing in the middle of the grand hall with her hands wide up in the air while Carrabella and Brenn are frozen in midair in front of her with canines showing.

We all gape stunned for a moment. If it was anyone else other than my sister in-laws I would probably laugh at their comical faces. Now there is no denying Issy is a witch even though she claims not to be. At that exact moment of realization I acknowledge my brother's protests from behind me.

"What the hell is going on here?" Maximus spats taking huge strides towards Carrabella.

"Bloody hell, let them down!" roar's Treyvon.

I put my hand high in the air, "Zip it!" I command in my older brother who demands respect and you best damn well pay attention voice.

"Ladies," I say to my brother's Eternalmates as I walk slowly between them snapping Issy, out of the trance she is in. I gently take a hold of her hand pulling her behind me strategically placing my body between hers and my family. Carrabella and Brenn both land on their feet in a fighting stance and jump back looking startled and ready to battle. Meanwhile my brothers run to their assistance wrapping their arms around them as the girls try to struggle away.

"Witch," proclaims Carrabella, ready to rip Issy's head off her neck if the fierce scowl on her face is any indication. She's ready to fight. Maximus moves his arms tighter around her waist smirking; I swear he likes this kind of shit. He holds her still his head leaning down over her shoulder. "Down baby," I hear him whisper to her. "I'll explain later."

"But she's a witch!" Carrabella says startled, "And she...she used magic against us Maximus!"

"Shh...I understand baby, but trust me it'll be alright." Maximus comforts Carrabella glaring at me.

"You know her Marcus?" Brenn asks shocked and confused.

I nod. "She's my guest."

"I'm so sorry; you didn't tell us you had a house guest, so we assumed she was a thief sneaking around your house peaking around corners." Brenn apologized anxiously while all of them eyeballed Issy up and down causing my temper to almost snap. Realizing her mistake Brenn says, "oh, oh I'm so sorry ...I I!" she tries to amend, but finally stops talking all together looking down. Treyvon spares her by taking her hands and leads her to the back of the room; her face is beat red as it should be. The woman ran a psychiatric facility before hooking up with Treyvon; you'd think she would be more skilled at this sort of negotiations. I guess in her defense she was taken by surprise, though.

I leer at them in disbelief before turning my eyes to Issy's. Her whiskey browns are wide and full of humility. She peers down at the ground all though her shoulders are still held high. I'm instantly for the first time in my long life ashamed of my own clan judging her by her appearance alone. It only strengthens my vow to protect Issy at all cost even with my own life.

"I I I don't understand what happened. Please forgive me," she apologizes to my brother's women cow eyed, "I heard women's voices and peaked out to see what was going on. I did not mean to harm you!" She states forcefully before taking a calming breath. "They called me a thief and tried to grab me. Before I could control it they were up in the air and I couldn't move." She adds looking at me her eyes wide and beckoning us to forgive her.

"It's ok. No harm, done except their pride which they'll get over. It's my fault, if anyone's to blame. If I had told them I had a house guest and introduced you sooner, this would not have happened. I beg your forgiveness," I tell her trying to relieve some of the tension in the room.

Sticking two fingers under her chin I lift it up until her eyes are square with mine and give her the softest feather light kiss across her lips, startling her.

She gasps, embarrassed. I lace my fingers with hers smile at her for reassurance turn and introduce her to my clan.

"Family this is Issy." Their mouth's all hang open. It's not their fault. I don't bring women around my clan. Why should I? They were never more than a fling. Not till this one. I will never forget the way there faces appear right now. I wish I'd thought to take a snapshot. "Issy this is my Clan." They all nod and one by one proper introductions are finally met.

"First of all this is Maximus and his Eternalmate Carrabella, or Carra, as some like to call her."

Their eyes cast away from each other's long enough to nod before flashing straight back to one another once again as Maximus kisses her. Copycat is all I can think.

"Next is Treyvon or Trey, as Brenn likes to call him. As you probably guessed already he is Maximus twin identical except for the color of their eyes obviously. Brenn is his girlfriend standing beside him."

"I'm so sorry about, well - everything. There is no excuse for my actions. In other words it's good to make your acquaintance." Brenn says while Treyvon grins and nods, but I can tell he's irritated I didn't introduce Brenn as his Eternalmate.

I can't help it if she hasn't claimed him yet, poor guy. For your Eternalmate not to claim you must be unbearable for him. Once a vampire even one who takes the blood pill finds his match it is customary and a primal need to claim them immediately to keep other men away. I wouldn't envy what Treyvon would do to any man who tried though. This is why he sticks like bonding glue to her side. Everyone realizes their Eternalmates either way, but we will respect her wishes until she finally comes around and shares blood with him and performs the marriage ritual.

"No, please – I understand perfectly," says Issy.

"These other two are the younger brothers, James and Anthony." I point to each of them in turn. "James is a seer, so don't be surprised if he all of a sudden tells you your future."

"Oh, good to know," she says nervously with a smile that never reaches her eyes. I don't think she likes the idea of someone seeing into her future or her past.

"Don't scare the girl Marcus," James says tight lipped talking to me than his attention turns to Issy and his whole demeanor changes, "If I get any premonitions about you I'll only tell you if you ask me too, or if its life threatening." states James with an arched brow trying to lure her in and my chest instantly gets a burning sensation that almost sends me to my knees and my hands tighten into fists. Damn him.

"Oooow!" Issy cries out. I glance down immediately realizing I had crushed her fingers entwined with mine. Shit!

"Oh, pardon me. Are you ok?" I say releasing her fingers and trying to see if I had broken any of them.

'Um, yeah, sure, it just took me off guard." She says looking at me skeptically like she's thinking 'what the fuck you almost crushed my fingers?' For the first time in my life as I peer up at my clan I acknowledge a slight blush brush over my skin. I clear my throat as they all grin a cats got your tongue kind of grin. Damn, I won't live this down for centuries.

"Ok, James, I'll keep that in mind," Issy says looking away not making eye contact with him or me and I'm relieved for the attention to be off me, but if I'm reading her correctly she's hoping it will stop James from having any premonitions about her. She must not realize he can't summons them at will.

"If you need help with anything electronics, Anthony's your man." I add continuing introductions wanting to be through already.

"I don't own a laptop or anything, but my alarm clock on this wrist watch often gives me a lot of trouble." She says pointing at her watch on her right wrist.

"I'd love to check it out if you'd like." Anthony purrs giving her a flirting heated stare causing me to want to knock it off his face. Jeez am I going to need to kill my brothers today?

I clear my throat. "Well there's no time for it now is there."

"It'll only take..." Anthony starts to say, but I give him the evil eye warning him he's stepping over boundaries better left untouched.

"What are we all doing loitering up here? I need to refresh my drink." Maximus says walking towards the stairs with his hand at Carrabella's back leading the way.

"Yes good call Maximus. Let's go back to my study and freshen our drinks. Then we need to simulate a plan to destroy these monsters. I don't like them being in our town prepared to hurt innocents."

"We won't let that happen," remarks Maximus.

"Yeah we will find them one by one and destroy them if we need too," Treyvon adds. Then it dawns on me this was also Brenn's home town not to mention the fact Carrabella and Maximus strong attachment to this area as well. After all this was the last place Carrabella lived before the curse was finally revoked and Crucia put behind bars where he belongs. Once were settled back down stairs Issy gives us the rundown.

"The hunters names are Matthew, Mark, Luke, John & Leviticus," states Issy with her lips turned up in an unnatural haunted grin. It sends shivers down my spine which is also unnatural. "Or so I call the five," she adds wrapping her hair behind her ears as she gets up and starts to pace the floor. "The only way to destroy them is for all evil to be gone. We all realize my mother tried to do a good thing, but it's never going to happen. It's not possible."

"We'd need to destroy the earth first." says Maximus.

"Which means we'd all be dead." confirms Issy.

"There must be another way," I offer.

"The only other way I've discovered after hours of researching on the computers at libraries, and several anonymous phone calls to covens around the world, is for the curse to be revoked." Issy adds grabbing a banana off the fruit bowl and sitting down beside me. Her body so close it sends a swift little tingle straight through my body and to my groin and I fight the urge not to grab her by the waist throw her over my shoulders and run up the stairs cave man style. I stand up instead and walk over to the bar trying to hide the tent forming in my jeans and pour me a glass of Treyvon's homebrew, needing something a little stronger.

"The problem is most spells need the witch who cast the spell to revoke it. Which might be an impossible task in this case since she was blown into smithereens by your mother a century ago? That is if I got the facts straight," remarks Anthony as he turns my way for confirmation.

I nod. "Unfortunately we found out the hard way about breaking curses with Crucia's curse."

"True that." My brothers agree in unison.

"And if we want to get technical about it both women put a spell on the hunters and both women are dead." I add between clenched teeth looking at Maximus who is now rummaging through my CD's. He ignores me, probably not wanting to think about breaking any more curses to the extent any of the rest of us do.

"The last curse because of a lot of complications took us four centuries to revoke. Crucia was a crafty character and much to our surprise had been using damn voo-doo dolls the whole time to steal Carrabella from us," states Treyvon.

"Crucia's curse?" Issy asks with a furrowed brow.

"Long story." I say looking from Maximus back to her and back again hoping she'll get the picture.

"Oh." She whispers under her breath.

"I'll explain later." I murmur quietly.

She shakes her head understanding. "So what you're saying is the spell can't be revoked?" Issy asks worried.

"Not unless you practice necromancy." Replies Treyvon.

I roll my eyes at Treyvon. "We will destroy them instead."

"Impossible. They can't be killed. I tried everything imaginable." Issy spats thumbing her chest. "They keep on going and going like that damn pink energizer bunny on the commercials!"

"Issy, everything can be destroyed even us immortals. We will figure out a way." I say patiently as if talking to a child which she is compared to me.

"I'll hop on my laptop when we're done here and find out what I can about them." Anthony adds writing something on his iPad. Anthony is our technical geek in the family and we're all more than happy to leave him to it. None of the rest of us seems to be inclined to do it ourselves.

"There is another possibility." States Maximus as he walks over to my cd player to pop in some tunes. He chooses American music so different from our own, but a nice change when you want something more contemporary. Hmm, 'Rhapsody Queen Bohemian,' good choice, but I hope they don't do what they usually do when this song is played and bust out in song. I quickly give them a warning glare when I see their lips about to sing 'Mama oooh ooh ooh.' Afterwards he walks over to my bar and pours himself a drink from the bottle of homebrew Treyvon had the decency to bring me from our homeland in the Carpathian Mountains, predicting I'd be out. He always gets the good stuff, but won't tell anyone who his suppliers are.

"Are you planning on sharing this with us?" inquires Anthony irritated brown eyes staring a hole through Maximus back. Putting into words what we all were thinking. Maximum's temper is nasty so most of the time we all let him alone not wanting to piss him off. It wasn't always so he used to be charismatic, outgoing, getting along with everyone he met, but Crucia did a number on him and left his mark. Fact is he did a number on all of us. None of us came out of that situation the same. We all blamed ourselves for not being able to keep Carrabella safe or figure out how Crucia was taking her. It's gotten a little better now that Carrabella and Maximus are reunited hopefully for good this time, but it didn't help for me to drag them here when they only want to be alone right now. Their intent is to spend the rest of eternity on a honeymoon. I believe he had a hundred year 'Do Not Disturb' sign, on his door when he got my message to come. Why Anthony is choosing now to upset him I don't understand.

Maximus turns our way takes a drink of his brew nice and slow, lets it settle, gives Anthony a sinister glare and says, "Hold you're horses. Not all men are like the feminine gender, so quick with their tongue. Some like to think things out first."

"Hey!" Issy protests under her breath as her spine stiffens, offended and I don't blame her. Maximus has been on this earth too long to say them kind of fighting words in front of a woman and not expect consequences.

Things happened quickly.

"Did you call me a pussy?" Anthony spats standing up ready for action and oh for crying out loud is all I can think, can they act any more juvenile?

Maximus leans against the counter getting comfortable like he doesn't have a care in the world. "If it suits you little brother action speaks louder than words, but anytime you think you're capable - I'm standing right here." He even grins, bringing his hands out level in front of him palms up fingers moving back and forth. "I'm all yours come and get me." He says answering my question, yes they can.

"Asshole," Anthony retorts. Thumb in the air pointing towards the door. "Let's take it outside." he growls as though they're sixteen and not five hundred years of age.

Issy flashes her eyes at me-as they fly towards each other bumping chests her foot doing the shaky thing they do when she's nervous. "Are they for real?" she finally asks.

I smile rolling my eyes and shaking my head up and down. "Now you understand why I'm here on an extended vacation!" I bark as they reach the door chests shoved together fists flying as Maximus kicks the French door open almost breaking the stained glass windows. "Get serious you two and mind your mouths in front of the lady. You can kick each other's butts later. Something I'd be more than happy to assist with I might add. But for now... we need to come up with a plan to stop these hunters!"

"There you go again ruining all the fun Marcus," Treyvon pipes in chuckling. "I thought we were going to get a real show." He rubs his hands together back and forth a couple of times barely sticking the tip of his tongue out of his lips biting down lightly a habit he's had since he was a baby like he was looking forward to a fight. He was probably planning on joining in like us brothers like to do sometimes for fun, but Issy doesn't need to discover those kind of brotherly facts so soon. There is nothing like an ass whooping amongst brothers. I take a deep breath.

"Okay fine party pooper. We were trying to let some steam off. It was a long boring airplane ride." Marcus states dryly before getting back on task. "So what if we were to get help from this Demigods parents, do we know who they are or if they had a good relationship with her?"

I shrug looking towards Issy.

"Perhaps we could get them to assist us. They might like this chapter of their lives ended as well. They are Gods after all which means their powers are limitless. My hunch is they will reverse it." Maximus adds scratching his chin looking skeptical grasping at straws, dark eyes deep in thought. So deep I can actually catch the wheels turning fine pointing his options. "You did say Lily's friend was a Demigod, what was her name?"

"Meredith," answered Issy and me at the same time.

"Ok, I thought so. Meredith had actually manipulated their minds in the first place right?"

"Yes!" Issy and I blurt out at the same time again. Our eyes flash at each other and we can't help, but laugh. I love the sound of our laughter as it intertwines dancing together in the air and throughout the walls of my house as though we've been doing it together all our lives, and it becomes music to my ears. Whoa... what am I thinking?

"Do the Gods realize Meredith is dead," Asks James?

"I was about to as the same question." says Maximus. "From what I'm told time goes by much quicker up there and a hundred years is like a blink of an eye to them."

"I've discovered the same," says James.

"So you're saying I need to get hold of Meredith's mother, or grandfather?" asks Issy, hope dawning in her eyes.

"Absolutely not," I retort slamming my glass to the table as all eyes turn to me alarmed!

"Why...?" asks Issy.

"What if they're not aware of her demise, and therefore becomes angry when we enlighten and decide to take it out on you, since Lily was your mother after all." I answer.

"Oh, I never thought of that," she murmur's with her whiskey colored eyes opened big and round.

"Well, it is a possibility." agrees Maximus shaking his head.

"On the other hand it could work in the opposite direction and perhaps their reaction could be of relief we educated them, so they could reverse what had happened?" prompts Anthony.

"I agree Anthony; it sounds like her Grandfather loved her even more than his own daughter. It may well please him instead of making him angry," adds James.

"In your dreams what grandfather would be relieved to receive news of his granddaughters death? What's wrong with the lot of you?" horror fills me at the thought. "Do you actually think somewhere in those thick skulls of yours I would take such a chance with Issy's life." I spat with a menacing growl, glaring at all of them in turn as they all stare at me as though I'm suddenly dressed in clown clothes with a big red rubber nose on my face.

"It's not your choice," whispers Issy under her breath bringing my attention back to her.

"No, and that's final. We'll find another way to break the curse or destroy them!" I snarl my chest doing the weird burning sensation again at the thought of what the Gods could do to her.

"Okay, point taken so how about this, would it be too much to venture we could trick the hunters into believing they had destroyed all the evil," he puts up quote signs, "as in anyone with unnatural powers unlike their own which would include, but not be limited to witches, werewolves, sorcerers, fae, angels, Demigods, vampires and any other unnatural species living on earth. It could be endless for crying out loud." Marcus says lifting his hand and rolling his eyes before adding, "Or do they want you in particular?" he stares at Issy, eyebrow raised intense brown eyes assessing hers expecting an answer. Her body crumbles a little before straightening her shoulders once again.

"I'm not sure, but yeah it seems personal." She answers rubbing her hands together obviously unsure of herself under his dark perusal. And it pisses me off at him. "I mean... the same scenarios been happening for so long..." she continues, "I run and hide. I can't be sure of whom else they hunt. I watched in horror as they killed my mom and I witnessed Zookie telling the story of how they murdered my father to my mom. One by one as my family tried to protect me they killed the rest of my coven, I mean family." she chastised herself, "one by one they staked each family member burning them alive while searching for me." She says rubbing her eyes head pointed down as if she's interested in her feet. I long to slip my arms around her, I want nothing more than to comfort her and take all of her worries away, but I resist not wanting the others to think she is weak and needing my assistance. There's nothing worse than showing weakness for our kind.

"Interesting ideas Maximus," I say annoyed getting up and walking over to the entertainment center wanting to get the attention off of Issy. I reach down to my cd player turning down the volume of the music, wondering if the other woman are done unpacking so we could take a ride into town and check it out. Tired of talking I get this antsy movement in my gut needing to be outside and searching for these hunters already. "I'd like to fly in to town and see how things are going. You guys think your women are getting close to settling in? Do you think they'd like to go with us or rest here for a spell?" I ask giving them the option.

"Nice try Marcus, but Carrabella will be coming with me. I'll message her to speed them up." Say's Maximus. No surprise there.

"I'm sure Brenn will want to go with us too. Knowing her she's probably already called all of her friends in town and will want to check in on them, besides she'll want to see Sophia and Buck. She was commenting about eating one of Buck's famous burgers on the way here." Answers Treyvon.

"Ok, well I think we've about discussed all we can for now. Let's think on it a spell and see what we can come up with while were in town."

"Marcus, I can tell you about Meredith's parents and their relationship. I met them as a child." Say's Issy out of the blue. Damn, she's not going to let sleeping dogs lie.

"I said no." I repeat with my back turned to hers. It wouldn't be wise to view her eyes when I comprehend the pleading in her voice.

"I understand what you said, but I could still tell you about them and perhaps we could do a little investigating. It's feasible. Couldn't we just find out?" she asks again.

"What good would it do?" I ask her still not turning her way, but boy oh boy I can feel the heat of those eyes on me as though she was touching the back of my neck and goosebumps automatically form and spread across my shoulders. Whiskey brown surrounded by green with the golden flicks, I memorized each one.

"I don't know. I think it would help me to find out for sure." She says all innocently, but I'm afraid she's planning something I'm not going to like.

"I can't stop you from telling us Issy, hell, it might even come in handy on figuring out how to kill the hunters. But I'm done discussing this Issy. I won't chance them finding out we're asking questions about them. They could get angry and come after you." I say trying to scan inside her head wondering how our connection is so strong. I want to discover if I can read her thoughts or only imagine I can. Not the everyday kind of mind reading I can do on mortals, but the blood only kind. After the mind blowing sex we had earlier the connection so strong it was as if we were one, mind, body and soul. Too strong to be considered casual sex. Oh no, this was special - like cannons shooting into the skies sex. Could this woman be my Eternalmate?

Nah, it's not possible. She's not a pure blood as far as she let on. I am a first born son, first generation from our village in the Carpathian Mountain and I will marry no one other than a pure blood. She will be a strong woman from our village line. A woman who went through all the pain, suffering, loss, changes we had to endure all those centuries ago. A woman who understands all the sacrifices and hard decisions our families had to make. The most important decision was of whether to be turned into the beasts that had attacked and killed most of our village. The beasts we are now. The woman for me needs to understand these facts and feel in her soul the same way I do. She has to believe and inforce our code of honor to never hurt humans. We are their sworn protectors as long as we draw breath. Issy is at least half witch and the trouble is I don't recall what their code is.

So the problem is she's more than likely not from our linage as far as I can tell, but I still can't help but wonder ... what if? Enough, I need to quit thinking of her this way. It will do neither of us any good. I decided my path of which I'd marry a long time ago and made a vow to only choose a pureblood. It was casual sex. That's all.

As if...I'm such a fool, is it even possible now since my hands caressed her skin, sampled her sweet lips and had her chest rise and fall beneath mine? Shit, what am I going to do now?

Issy brings me back to the conversation by shaking her nervous foot next to mine. I harden my thoughts when I peer up at her and am surprised to find she seems to discover the difference immediately. Her eyes widen briefly as if I had reached out my hand and slapped her across the face or as if she listened to every word I was thinking. She leans back further into the couch closes her eyes for a moment rubbing her lids with her hand then removes her hand and her face is determined as she answers my question as if nothing had occurred between us. But one thing for sure is a whole hell of a lot happened between us, and well, it kind of freaks me out to be so in tuned to Issy.

"Well, I can't be stifled so easily and I think if you'd just listen mayhap I can talk some sense into that stubborn head of yours."

"Woman you haven't seen stubborn yet."

"Marcus their family wasn't close."

"Okay, I get that but how does this help our situation?"

"Meredith's mother was the God of light, her father a human. Meredith and her mother never seen eye to eye. She blamed her mother for her father's strange and untimely death."

"Why did she blame her mother?" asks Maximus.

"She didn't understand the concept of why her mother Celeste, hadn't saved her father Sampson, and turned him into an immortal like them."

"Well it is a good question. Why didn't she turn her husband? Did he choose not to be turned?" asks James. "From what I remember my mom telling me Celeste had confided in her. She shared Sampson had been evil from the start and had tricked her in the first place to make her fall in love with him. He was full of deceit and only wanted her so he could try and steal her powers."

"Like father, like daughter it would seem." remarks James.

"Well under those circumstances no wonder she didn't save him." I say.

"The real question is did she kill him?" asks Treyvon.

"No way man, my guess is it was her father who killed him." says Maximus.

"No, but nice try, her father got wind of what Sampson was up to and sent him out of the realm. The only reason he hadn't killed Sampson was because he was his grandchild Meredith's, father. This caused a lot of disturbance in the heavenly realms and he never forgave Meredith's mother Celeste, for her part in that."

"Ok, but you didn't answer the question of who killed Sampson?" said Maximus.

"The funny thing is his death had nothing to do with any of them. His death was on his own accord dealt from some underhanded people he had been dealing with here on earth, from what she said. So you see they weren't close at all. My bet is her mom would want to help us end this once and for all." Issy finished eyes sad for a moment before they clear and turn dead serious as though she's come to some internal decision.

I nod wanting to placate her because her eyes are glossed and her lips are set in a pout. Pretending to accept what she said as possible for the mean time even though my gut is screaming this plan won't work and there is no way in hell I will jeopardize her.

She takes a breath and then adds standing up rubbing her hands up and down her hips in an anxious way, "Now, are we done? Your mind is made up Marcus, and well, so is mine so it's time...well what I mean is I need to move on." Leaving me for the first time in my life flabbergasted! My molars pop. She turns and walks towards the door.

Instead of following her I say, "If you think it's a good idea Issy. I can't stop you, but where will you go? Those monsters are still out there close to my land - waiting for you. Your car is gone Issy. Tell me how will you escape this time?" She stops dead in her tracks. Victory is at hand; At least for now. Even if I can't claim her, I won't let her leave. It's too dangerous for her now. She turns and walks up the stairs without saying another word. My gut quivers going sour. Sure, I won, but at what price? My head is thundering into my eardrums and all I want to do is run to her.

8

Memories

Issy

$\mathcal{I}$ walk back into, Marcus room slowly, hurt and confused. I had witnessed the change in, Marcus, immediately. It was as though he had made his mind up about us, and it was final. What caused this change of heart I'm not sure, but I'm damn well going to find out. It was evident by the scare tactic he chose. The perfect words, 'they're still out there just beyond my property line.' However his words are not why I stayed, but he doesn't need to find that out quite yet. I chose to stay because in his own way he was pleading for me to stay, and I could barely make out the slight tone in his voice saying, he would be devastated if I left.

Well, two can play at his game. If he thinks he can stay away from me, and keep me around at the same time as in, 'have his cake and eat it too', than he'll learn he's wrong the hard way I decide sitting on the bed crossing my arms over my lap. He took my virginity and I'm not letting him go. My mother told me as a little girl to save my most precious part of me as long as I can. When I shared this gift, among gifts, to make sure it was given to someone I loved, and respected, and wanted to be with the rest of my life. A tad bit old fashion for this day and age I realize, but I've never found anyone that had interested me in the way, Marcus does. He shook me to the core. Mom told me to make sure above all else he was good, kind, strong willed, courage's yet fair. That man is, Marcus.

All this talk about my mother stirs up old memories from long ago, another time really, my mind slips further into the past it was the day my father was murdered in cold blood. I had witnessed my mom and her closest friend Meredith talking quietly.

They seemed upset, but trying to keep whatever they were talking about a secret from me. I'm not sure why this concerns me it's not like they're not always keeping secrets from me however this time something is irrevocably wrong. I shiver as though a bunny jumped over my grave, as the saying goes, and cross my arms rubbing them trying to stir some friction up to bring life back into them again.

From out of nowhere my mom lets out a terrifying sound coming straight from her gut and out her mouth grabbing her stomach and falling to the ground as though she was in terrible crippling pain. I try to run towards her, but before I could reach her my aunt grab's a hold of me holding me back firmly in place while, Meredith fell to the ground hugging my mother. But for some reason I don't understand my mom wasn't having it. She actually tensed and did something I've never seen her do before. She screamed for, Meredith not to touch her, eyes streaming with tears and outrage. Unexpectedly she takes it even further pointing towards the door and bellowing for, Meredith to get out of her house and never return. I stiffen. Meredith is my mom's dearest friend, what is going on?

Meredith peered at my mom with tear filled eyes, begging her to let her stay. "Please, please don't do this Lily, please! It wasn't my fault, I beg you, I am only the bearer of bad news!" she cried.

"You lie!" my mother yelled. "He warned me not to trust you. He told me you were jealous and had flirted with him many times trying to turn his mind against me and instead be with you. He told me you were not what you seemed."

"No, tis not true." Meredith, tried to defend herself.

"You lie, you had something to do with this, I can feel it in my bones." My mom yelled, as she pulled herself up from the floor turned and took off running out of the room. The sound of her footsteps running down the hall up the stairs and into her room as the door slammed behind her gave me the chills. I acknowledge her loud screams and whelps of unimaginable pain, and realize they were tears of grief.

Meanwhile, Meredith got up from the floor, straightened her dress, patted her hair walked over to the coat rack, grabbed her cloak threw it over her shoulders, and looking scornful stomped out of the house muttering, "You'll be sorry for this, Lily."

Afterwards my aunt let go of me and took off running in the same direction my mom had ran. I crept slowly, quietly, following her steps, not wanting to give myself away. One way or another, I'm going to get the truth. The pit of my stomach was raw, and churning, whatever happened to my father, was going to change my life forever. She disappeared into my parent's room closing the door. I crept to the door and leaned my ear against it listening for every sound. At first she was soothing mama... "Now, now it will be OK. Let it out." it went on for quite a while before she finally started getting any real answers out of her.

"Lily, what's happened?" No answer, only more sobs. "Is it word of James?" she continued in a soothing voice. "Is he dead?" My mother let out a loud sob of grief once more. My father is hurt badly in some remote spot even my coven couldn't get to him, which is almost impossible, or dead.

Otherwise mama would be searching for him, instead of lying on the floor freaking out. It came over me like a tidal wave, the pain rippled from every cell of my body, and like my mother I slid to the floor in a paralyzed state not able to move, or speak, or cry. My father wasn't coming home ... There was no more denying the fact!

I lay on the cold floor for what seemed like hours but I'm sure we're only mere moments. He had disappeared days ago with no word he was leaving. Not like him. Not like him at all. My parents had a loving close relationship and they told each other everything. I'm the only one who gets told lies. For my protection I'm told, but I don't want to be lied to either way.

Sometime in the night aunt Callie tried pushing on the door to get out of her room, but instead hit up against my sleeping lifeless body waking me from the supine position I was in. She leaned down kissing my forehead tears still wet in her eyes. "I thought I'd find you here. Come with me, I'll put you to bed in my room tonight. You're mamma needs time to rest and think." I laid my head on my auntie's as she carried me to her room. All sorts of thoughts we're reeling through my mind. One in particular was why was mom so mad at Meredith her closest friend? Why did she push her away and make her leave.

It's not like my mother to raise her voice at anyone. I don't understand what's going on, and I already miss my father so much its painful, what happened? Why won't anyone ever tell me what's really going on... must I always walk through this world in the dark, not knowing?

I cry myself to sleep with the unshed tears I had been holding in, mourning whatever happened knowing it is detrimental to our future. Fearing the worst my father is dead, and Meredith the demigod had something to do with it.

Someone's shaking me and I try to ignore it enjoying my slumber until I realize it's my mother trying to wake and dress me simultaneously. "Shh... make no sound- we're leaving. We're being hunted by bad people." Her eyes are dead serious and even at my young age I know when her eyes are wide with a piercing glare and her face is hard as stone, she means business.

"Do you understand Issy? Not one sound!" she put her index finger to her lips in a Shh motion. Her voice is stern. My mother will kill to protect me of that there is no doubt.

"Witch hunters," my aunt exclaims bursting back into her room grabbing her cloak and throwing it over her shoulders. Looking at us, she whispers, "We must leave now-ready?" My mother nods and they both grab my hands while grabbing each other's - we are in a circle "...one ...two ...three." And poof, the next thing I know we all tumble through the air in a secret passage, round and round we go. I recall traveling through it before when I was much younger, but still it takes me off guard, causing my stomach to lurch as we land on a familiar hill. We roll to our feet in a group my mother and aunt catching me before I fall. Both of them land in a fighting stance legs spread hands held high ready to defend us if they need to.

My mom abruptly turns to the south, "whose there?" she hisses forcefully! Her eyes on fire, face hard lined muscles bunching, lips tight.

A man takes a step out from under the trees and right away I recognize our grounds keeper and friend Zookie. "Come quick, I brought a wagon!" he instructs almost reluctantly, I'm only a kid but I see the hesitance in his eyes. What's he doing here, or better yet, who told him we were going to be here? My auntie probably planned this with Zookie beforehand is all I can guess?

The three of us start to follow Zookie, when mom abruptly raises her hand commanding, "halt!" We all stop turning to her. "Where are the others?" She demands, long red blond hair blowing in the wind, hands by her sides loose and ready to use if she needs too.

My auntie agrees brown eyes slanting, "Yes...Zookie, where is the rest of our clan?"

I spot the sweat glistening on his dark skin and the muscles in his cheeks clenching tight. Zookie was acting odd, even to me a child. His eyes like dark deep pools of death, instead of happy and full of laughter like they usually did, and before anything else could be said Zookie grabs a hold of me, he has me positioned in front of him sticking a sharp knife to my neck. I gasp. The blade is cold and I tremble my legs turning lifeless. Totally out of the blue it's urgent that I go pee. Oh no...I mustn't. Wide eyed I looked at my mom trying to prevent the tears. Mom and Aunt Callie step forward simultaneously raising their hands.

"Stop right there," Zookie orders with a stern voice, "don't make me kill her, Lily!"

I gasp.

"You dare threaten Lily's daughter, Zookie?" My aunt, Callie spats outraged with the hint of death to come in her voice.

My mom puts her hand up, "Zookie, what did she do to you?" Her eyes are not angry anymore but soft - a tear slips down from her right eye trickling down her cheek. The pressure on the knife to my neck slightly loosens. Before I can even think of the relief building, my aunt blasted him away from me - slamming him against a tree where Zookie slides to the ground with blood dripping from his lips and is immediately knocked out. Tears fill my eyes. I don't know if there for Zookie or because I am saved.

My mom runs to me throwing one arm around my shoulder the other hand goes to my neck as her eyes search for any signs of damage, while my aunt goes to check on, Zookie. Zookie opens his eyes and chokes on the blood slipping out of his mouth. His eyes clear to his normal appearance.

"Meredith cast a spell on the witch hunters, to get them to kill, Johnathon. They tricked him. They murdered him in cold blood. Staking him they tore out his heart Lily, I'm so sorry. They pieced it up and shared it amongst the five of them eating it while, Meredith looked on with a sadistic smile on her face. She had laughed a cold, devilish sound coming and then cackled you were next. She and her Hunters are coming for you too. She threatened my family Lily. Run...Run all of you." he croaked. "She won't stop until every one of you are dead!" he closes his eyes as his head plops back against the tree.

"Dead," Callie says, picking up his hand, dropping it again as we stare at them open mouthed. "What a waste." she adds, nose scrunched up in disgust, rubbing her hands on her long black skirt tails, as if touching Zookie had dirtied her hands as she walks towards us. She doesn't mean it at all though. I don't think it's possible, she's too angry for remorse. He had threatened me and that was all she cared about. My aunt, Callie holds a fierce grudge and she always gets even in the end. Mom holds on to me soothingly for a moment, while my aunt scopes things out around us with the, 'mind thing,' her and my mom can do. It's like they possess a crystal ball and can see what's happening all around them and sometimes into the future. They don't though...I know... being the curious child that I am I've searched every nook and cranny. They tell me it's nothing, secrets again...always more secrets. But I can tell they're different from others...and so am I. The power that lies inside of me is getting stronger every day, begging for release.

Marcus glorious scent of sandalwood and Old Spice fills my nostrils bringing me back to the here and now, and I stiffen my spine.

9

Town

Marcus

My brothers and I finish our plans assigning each person to their own duties and take a break for nourishment before starting for town.

The women are still getting settled so I take a moment to myself needing to think by walking outside and disposing of the garbage. Too much is happening too fast. Witch hunters which seem to be hunting everyone but mortals, and even the mortals aren't safe from them. From what Issy told us these so called 'do gooders,' will trample anyone to get what they want.

Issy mentioned these monsters had staked her father. Torn his heart out with their grubby little hands, diced it up in five pieces and shared it between the five of them. And they call us the monsters, I think with a low whistle. They sacrificed these people before the curse had even been placed on them. My guesstimate is this is the hunter's way of telling us we aren't coming back once they destroy us. It could be a delicatessen to them, hell I don't know. However, we are not going to let it happen to us.

Then there's, Issy sweet yet strong. I'm unable to keep my mind from straying to her. Even now I wonder what she's doing up there in my room all alone? There's no movement or sound besides her breathing. Which is something we only do out of habit it hasn't been necessary since the change.

It's still mind blowing to me how quickly she absorbed the change in me earlier and worse yet how she reacted to it. With a flash of my eyes I hurt her deeply; it's as if she read my mind by searching my eyes. This is usually something only an Eternalmate, blood family member, or someone you've shared blood with can do. Again this was odd because she's neither, but I can't scratch the memory.

There is the exception and that would be, James.

Of course, James power I think was a fluke accident, but who's to say. It was probably the fact the vampire who bit him was an original. James doesn't so much read minds as see visions of the past and future. If she does possess the power to read my mind it could be subtle, and she doesn't even realize what's happening to her. Especially since she denies being a witch, and tries to hold back the power I witnessed with my own eyes lies within her. Somehow I don't think this is the case.

Not able to take her absence any longer I appear behind her and what I find is almost more than I can bear. She sits on my bed, her tiny little shoulders crumpled in defeat. I can barely breathe almost crippled over by her sadness. What's wrong with my head is it screwed on backwards? How can I hurt this woman who gives me air... light... everything real? Even though we only met yesterday are union is so strong as though it's been forever. Why did I think I could live without her? There must be a way.

She stiffens her spine and turns her head towards me. My stomach lurches sickened by the hurt I see in her brown eyes, as her blondish red hair slides down into her cautious face. I put that caution there and I am ashamed. Love - hate so close. But I can change this for the better. I can make it up to her. I know I can if she'll only give me the chance.

"It's time to go." she say's snapping out of it, lifting her chin as if nothing ever happened.

"Yes, that's why I'm here."

"To escort me out, you afraid I'm going to steal something, Marcus?" she says arching her brow and lifting her stubborn chin.

"No, why would you ask me something like that, Issy?"

"You said that's why you're here."

"I came to tell you to get ready, were going to town now to scope things out. You still don't trust me, do you? I don't have any reason to think of you as a thief, even if you did snoop through my medicine cabinets. Your explanation had been more than enough for me to take you at your word.

"I'm sorry. I misunderstood you."

"I'd say?" I move towards her reaching out my hands. She stiffens.

"I'm ready, Marcus." her eyes are dark, serious, un-caring and it haunts me.

"To go to town, with me?"

"Yes, shall we?" She adds tight lipped her jaw firm as she tries to scoot around me towards the door.

"Issy," I murmur, voice cracking as she reaches for the door handle. I am overwhelmed, wanting to explain the change of heart, but the words fail me. I clear my throat.

"Let's get this show on the road." she uses a cliché looking back at me sternly, her brown eyes on fire now."

"Issy let me speak…"

"Don't you understand? I'm tired of running. I'm ready for this to end, Marcus. They destroyed and killed everyone who was and is dear to me. I want to kill these bastards!" she says not giving me a chance to speak. Her voice strong, but with hints of the real feelings I know surround her, protecting her, not willing to give her up quite yet. The lyric's, 'Then you might know what it's really like to have the blues,' play's in the background on the radio. Oh I so understand that song right now, I think, inhaling a deep breath.

I stare her straight in the eyes, careful, not giving anything away of my true thoughts, since it's obvious she doesn't care. "Ok, if that's what you want…let's ride." I growl using a cliché of my own. The man in me is screaming, 'sit her down and explain your thoughts to her,' but the hunter in me agrees with her, wanting nothing more than to kill those worthless hunters myself.

We ride into the sky the moon barely casting her shine, trees rippling in the slight wind enough to cool us off. The air is full of electricity and enthralls me to ride crazily through the air right on Issy's tail, whisk her off to a deserted island, where we can be alone and I can do wild things to her body. But I can't think that way. At least not now, when there is so much at stake, and so much I don't know about her.

We land a couple of miles out of town, and hike in which only takes a few seconds with our speed. We don't want the hunters to take notice, with this much power coming into town all at the same time.

Issy and I venture to the Shitkick bar. She is reluctant to come with me. "I need to know, Buck & Sophia are safe," I tell her, "and warn them of what's to come. We will enlist them to tell others coming in to the bar to go back home, call their friends and family, and inform them. The important thing is for everyone to stay home and out of sight. If what you tell me is true, and from what I witnessed with my own eyes last night, I believe it is, these hunters won't care who they kill to get what they want."

"No they won't. Where are the others going, Marcus? Are you sure we should separate? I'd fill terriblel if something were to happen to any of them."

"That's sweet of you, but I assure you they can take care of themselves."

"Okay, if you say so. However you don't understand what they're capable of like I do."

"They're all trained fighters they'll be fine. Now as far as the rest of my clan goes, Maximus and Carrabella are going to the library, and the sporting goods store. Anthony is headed to the electronics store. James thinks the city graveyard is his best bet. And last but not least Treyvon and Brittaney are going to the gateway to the Cascade National Forest, where you and I were last night. The same spot where the hunters were last seen all though I think it's pointless. The likely hood of them still at that location is null as far as I'm concerned, yet we still need to confirm. We will all gather at the Shitkick bar for dinner, when we've finished what we came here to do."

"Why are Maximus and Carrabella going to the sporting goods store?"

"To find any and all weapons so we can arm all mortals who are eligible to carry firearms, in case the monsters try to enter their homes, or are somehow able to destroy us. Highly doubtful, but stranger things happen all the time."

"Okay I see, and James, why the graveyard?"

"James is hanging out at the graveyard, waiting to see if any new dead come his way, hoping to speak with the receiving angel. I doubt he will see her, because they are only seen if they choose to be; besides I am still uncomfortable with this plan."

"Oh let's not start this again, Marcus."

"Fine, but I'm still not sure how they convinced me to go along with this. If your name is mentioned or you get hurt in any way because of this turn of events, there will be hell to pay for all of my brothers, and I'll be the one inflicting it!"

"Don't you trust your brothers?"

"With my life."

"Well then, quit worrying."

"Easier said than done, woman."

So far I don't see any noticeable signs the hunters are here, but the remnants of their raunchy disgusting odor still burns my sinuses from last night. I can't imagine that stench could be disguised. If they show up in town their odor will reach us long before we see them, is my thought. There could be another side to them able to hide in situations which call for it, like coming to town. The rest of us immortals are able to mask the signs of our true age, perhaps the same is true for them.

"It's still so hard for me to believe these hunters exist, besides been around hunting you and all other immortals for over a hundred years, without me ever hearing about them."

"They hide well."

"How can that be? From what I seen and smelt last night I can't imagine them able to hide their identities."

"Believe me Marcus they are masters at hiding."

"It would be a helluva lot better if we had some clue as to what powers they can wield. You say they can't be killed, but take it from me everything can be killed. We only need to determine how."

"You'll see soon enough. No one believes me Marcus. There unbelievable fast for their size and I'm not kidding when I say they CAN hide that stench."

Walking into the Shitkick bar we are immediately greeted by Sophia. "Well hello you two. It's good to see you again, Issy. You appear one hundred percent better compared to yesterday, dear." She hugs Issy first as though she were family and it warms me from the inside out before reaching for me smiling one of those cats got your tongue kind of smiles her lashes winking at me as though she knows something we are not aware of.

"Thanks," Says Issy, smiling sweetly at Sophia in return. "I'm happy to see you again too, Sophia."

"Did you get her car fixed, Marcus? Here, take a seat," she says ushering us to the bar and patting a bar stool.

Issy and I glance at each other and then say at the same time. "No, It wasn't fixable."

"Oh, well, it must be in bad shape, Marcus usually can fix anything with a motor." Sophia returns with a frown on her face.

"It's a long story." I intervene. "One I'll tell you and Buck in a bit."

"Oh, ok. Well, what will it be today, Marcus?" she asks patting her short black hair looking concerned. The woman though older in her fifties when she was turned is still a fine beauty. Her body still perfectly curved similar to a woman in her late twenties. Proof she exercised and ate right before she was brutally changed.

"Whiskey, and a quiet booth – I need to talk to you and Buck in private," I answer quietly looking her straight in the eye, speaking in an even tone letting her know this is serious and not to be taken lightly.

"Oh," she says in a questioning tone, nodding, understanding the importance of what I was about to tell them.

"How about you Issy," she asks green eyes shining with dread as she turns and leads us back and into her office deciding against the bar stool.

"Water," Issy answers quietly.

"Okay, I'll be back in a moment with Buck, your drinks and a menu." She say's winking at us with a smile which never reached her eyes, as she walks out the door leaving Issy and me alone.

I take the second nearest seat at the table expecting her to sit next to me. Issy on the other hand surprising me once again makes a point of walking all the way around the table to sit as far away from me as humanly possible, without leaving the room all together. A good idea, I guess. I don't think I can control myself to sit by her side and not touch her anyway, even now with so much at stake. Still it bothers me. She keeps her eyes everywhere, but at me only checking Sophia and Bucks office around her out. As though it's the most important thing she could do right now to memorize everything and its place. I try to speak, but nothing audible comes out. I clear my throat. And then it's too late.

Buck pushes through the door taking up most of the room with his bravado alone.

"What's happening, somethings in the air?" He demands anxious sitting my whiskey in front of me and the water in front of Issy. Buck is a big man, he was a lumber jack and probably as strong as five men even as a human.

"Wait for me," Sophia orders closing the door behind her, two more drinks in one hand I can only presume for her and Buck, and menu's in the other.

They both sit down and we explain the whole long sorted out story to them along with the plan A, B & C.

"Well I'll be damned Buck, you were right for once." Sophia says, to her Eternalmate wide eyed with a half menacing grin. She grabs her cell out of her apron pocket and says, "We need to start warning people and the fastest thing I can do right now is post it on Facebook and hope my friends and family will believe this crazy story and hit 'share'!"

"Yes, yes great idea Sophia, social media quicker than the news and the radio." Buck says, getting out of his chair walking towards his computer sitting in front of it and turning it on. "I'm going to put it on Facebook and twitter. I'll call the local radio and TV stations. Not that they will believe me, but it's worth a try all the same." He says determined to get the word out too.

Issy and I sit there staring at each other for a moment and I swear were thinking exactly the same thing, 'why didn't we think of that?' Social media of course everyone knows it's the fastest way to get the news out. My only hope is none of the five are on Facebook and this doesn't start an all-out panic amongst the people. We must be extremely careful of what is said.

I take my phone out of my pants pocket a little riled by Issy's unwavering stare as though once again she can see into my mind straight to the depths of my soul as I thumb my Facebook app. Next I send out a mental note to my clan to do the same.

A second later I get a message back from Anthony reading. 'I already thought of that. I'm setting up a home web page now. People will be able to reach us if they get any word of these hunters' whereabouts or are in need of our assistance. Also we will be able to warn them of the area these hunters are in as we get more accurate and up to date information. And hopefully will be able to get to these locations and destroy the hunters before they kill any innocents.'

'Good idea.' I message back and then inform the rest that Anthony will send out a message on Facebook and twitter with the address or link to get to this web page as soon as he's done creating it.

"Wow, I can't believe how fast this went viral," says Buck not even a half an hour later.

"Everyone is talking about it. It's even been shared on YouTube. Some people think it's a joke at first, but after careful consideration realize we don't joke about maters of life and death," say's Sophia.

"Yeah from what I gather many with good since are staying home and preparing to be in lock down for however long this takes to end. However others, the vigilante types are gathering weapons of all sorts' guns, knives, ropes, bullets, shovels, machetes, ak47, the list goes on and on. Basically anything they can find to use as a weapon in destruction.

They're getting themselves ready to go south of town and meet these witch hunters head on, Marcus," says Buck concerned.

"Damn, this is something in good conscience, I can't let them do." I say standing. "I understand their way of thinking, and admit I agree and want nothing more than to meet the hunters head on. On the other hand the problem with that is I've seen these monsters with my own eyes, and can only assume mortals wouldn't stand a chance against them."

"Yep, I figured you'd say that. What's the plan?" Buck says standing next to me ready to help. This is his town. He doesn't want blood shed any more than I do.

"I suppose we should head them off and turn them around."

"No problem, the place is slow today even without the news of the witch hunters. Sophia, baby, you got this right?"

"Of course I do. Be safe and turn those vigilantes around." Sophia says, walking up to Buck as he takes her in his arms and plants a kiss to her lips. My eyes wander to Issy. She's watching them with longing in her eyes. Does she want me to kiss her before we leave as badly as I want to kiss her, I wonder? How would she react if I tried with Buck and Sophia in the room? As if on cue she turns to me.

"I'm going too." She states.

"That's not necessary. Help Sophia run the place while we're gone instead."

"But..."

"Oh yes, thank you Issy, I'd love the help." Sophia says helping me out before Issy could refuse. "Come let me show you around. You'll wait the tables while I do the cooking..." She adds pulling Sophia towards the door.

"Yes, but I need to help..."

"Yes, thank you I am so grateful for your help." Sophia responds pulling her through the threshold.

I turn towards Buck, "Remind me to thank Sophia for that later, will ya?"

"Sure will. Now are we taking weapons and driving, or are we using are special talents and flying?"

"I'd like to take your Ford Raptor and it would set a better example, however time is of the essence and we need to find out what these vigilantes are planning before we confront them."

"Okay let me tell Sophia what's going on with the grub I've got started in the kitchen."

Ten minutes later we're south of town combing the grounds. "There, up ahead." I say flying into the trees overhead and landing on a branch.

"Idiots, do they really think their measly little barricade has the potential to keep these hunters out?" says Buck, landing beside me.

"There drinking too and getting rambunctious. At this point in time they'd probably shoot first and ask later to anybody wandering their way."

"Look at them wearing camo and sneaking around even while building a bon fire. There practically inviting the hunters to come and kill them."

"How many you reckon there are?"

"Seventy-five, maybe a hundred with more, on the way."

"Too many to hypnotize, and even if we got the local police and arrested them there would be no place big enough, except maybe the Concrete High School down river."

"How would we get them there?"

"Hell I don't know, school bus?"

"It could work, without any bloodshed."

"Let's use the strategic flanking maneuver."

"Right... heads or tails?" Buck says flipping a quarter into the air.

"Heads you're in the rear." I say watching him turn back in to his eagle form as I turn in to mine thinking this is going to be a hell of a lot of fun while wondering at the same time where the hell the hunters are now and hoping Issy is ok?

10

Receiving Angel

James

$\mathcal{I}$ wait at the grave side of Sedro Woolly's last victim of the angel of death. It's a few minutes after midnight and I've been waiting a while for the receiving angel to show. My luck she's late I think looking at my cell. From what I was told she was supposed to be here right at the stroke of midnight to pick up this poor soul. A young man of only twenty two, a life wasted and taken to soon only because of one of the many mortal drugs. He died years before his appointed death. Such an unfortunate waste if you ask me. If it were possible I would destroy all these drugs and end the struggle for so many people who are unable to stop using on their own.

Most of them go into it innocently enough. In most cases they are still in school anywhere from elementary school on. These drugs are presented to them at a time in their life when they are most vulnerable and going through hormonal changes.

Others are too rich or too poor and bored. They try the drugs at a party or even in the bathroom at a school, work, or church function, and wham one hit and they're hooked. They think these drugs make them invincible, taking all worries and insecurities away from them. Too soon they realize there is no control over it. They lie, steal, and anything else they need to do to get more drugs, even from their own family, coworkers, teachers and their priests. No-one is exempt. Sadly this is one of the leading reasons for crime and death in this modern world.

I'm so lost in thoughts I barely sense when the receiving angel finally shows her face. I gasp. Stumble away from her stunned at first. Oh my, and what a face it is. The woman is absolutely certifiably gorgeous! And what surprises me even more is the fact she is covered from head to toe in gold dust. I had heard of this beautiful receiving angel before, yet had not had the pleasure of meeting her until this night. The woman is actually glowing! Like a glow-worm my nephew play's with. Her blue eyes are wide, bright and intelligent. Everything else about her is covered in some sort of gold. I mean everything! Her lushes perfect curves, breast, shoulders, neck, face, mile high legs all covered in gold dust. She's not wearing real clothes, only a nylon skin sheer tight body glove of some type barely covering her lushes curves at all. It is all gold flaked and what makes it even more provocative is the fact it is a darker gold in the more private areas making it hard for me to advert my eyes! I am a man after all.

I stand there staring at the woman. She's an Aphrodite. Stunning doesn't even describe her.

"Are you done gawking at me sir?" she asks, annoyed if the narrowed eyes are any indication, and the sharpness of her tone. She moves her hand's with long darker colored golden tipped nails, to her hips. "I mean you would think an immortal would exhibit better manners." She snaps her fingers right in front of my face, snapping me out of my trance and I finally realize the goddess is talking to me. She's asking me questions no less.

"Oh, pardon me..." I say slightly uncomfortable, but she continues talking ignoring me.

"What are you doing out here anyway? Don't you use Facebook, or Twitter? It's all people are talking about - the witch hunters I mean."

"Witch hunters. Ahh... Yes, that's why I'm here." I say quickly, before she thinks I'm a mime and incapable of speaking.

"Well it's about time. What took you so long?"

"I'm not sure what you mean. I barely learned of them today." I say, curiously finding it extremely difficult to stay on subject and not let my eyes wander down her exquisite form.

"We've been waiting for you a long time. The souls are piling up. As soon as you free the hunters I can set them free. I'm running out of rooms for them." she say's, running her fingers down her golden hips as my eyes leisurely follow causing me to groan before it dawns on me what she had said.

I stiffen, perplexed. "Free the hunters? What are you talking about, woman? We're here to destroy the hunters, not free them!"

She gasps. Blue eyes widening mouth shaped in an O. "Kill them?"

"Yes, kill them. Why the hell would you think we were here to free them? Free them from what? My sources tell me they're already free wandering the earth killing innocents everywhere they go." Her face goes pale.

"If you're not here to free the witch hunters, why are you here interrupting my work?"

"I wanted to speak with you. Ask you a few questions if you don't mind." I answer, watching every sweet muscle on her beautiful face trying to judge how she's going to react. The last thing I want to do is anger this creature. "Word on the street is you're able to send a message to your realm addressed to the Gods. Is it true?"

"Only If I decide the message to be sent, is for a good enough cause."

"The reason for the message is a worthy cause, I assure you. I'm willing to trade for any favor you would like." I say hoping the favor she would want would be my body; boy howdy would I love to share it with her. Only in my wildest dreams would something so marvelous happen to me. A woman as striking as this one is must be taken already. She's an angel from another realm of all places. She died and went to heaven, whereas I come from the demons of hell. She wouldn't be interested in me an immortal doomed to walk the earth for eternity. Granted it's not my fault

I was turned into a vampire. I did not choose this way of life. I take the Hemocil to keep me as human as possible, nonetheless this beauty was sent back as an angel. I am a devil compared to her.

"Okay," she says decidedly her chin up in the air eyes measuring me, "just one question, if I send the text for you, what favor will I receive in return?"

I stare down at her in surprise.

"Well...speak your mind sir!" she demands. Her sweet succulent lips curl up in a smile which would make any man lose control. "That is if you dare!" she adds perkily her tongue flipping up to her top lip.

"My body," I purr my voice going a few octaves lower than usual never leaving eye contact with her.

I wait for the slap, but surprisingly it doesn't come. She struts around me like the angel she is. Standing in front of me again she stops taking a deep slow breath, leisurely looking my body up and down. She stops at the bulge she's created in my jeans, and then licks her sweet hot lips, I groan. Afterwards she makes me the happiest man in the world by reaching her hand out to shake mine.

"Deal, as soon as my work here is done. I'm extremely busy you know. Later we'll meet for a drink at the Shitkick bar. It's the closest one near the graveyard. Can your questions wait that long?" she adds cool and calmly looking at her gold tipped nails, as though none of this is affecting her at all.

I nod. My knees buckle for the first time in my life. I am so relived and a little surprised at the same time. My little angel might have a little bit of devil in her after all. And the woman has the audacity to giggle signaling me to the fact she is intuitive, too. I like...I like very much.

"I'll see you there about three am?" She nods. "Oh and umm....?" A blush. "Umm... This is awkward, but I don't know your name." she says with a grin wrapping her arms around her waist.

"I'll be damned if I don't know yours either." I chuckle. "My name is James, pleased to meet you," I say reaching my hand towards hers. "And yours is?"

"Mariah." She says still blushing, then ads, "By the way James, don't forget to drink your blood. You'll need the energy." She jests, winking as she reaches her sparkly hand out to my extended hand.

"Oh will I now?" I say, grinning like a little kid with a brand new bike wanting to take her now and I would if it wasn't for the poor young soul she needs to transport to his final destination. I grasp on to her hand bring it to my lips and brush it against her knuckles.

"Uh huh, we angles are brimming over with stamina." She whispers, as she turns to do her work promptly excusing me. As if she doesn't know what affect she's had on me. The vixen, at this rate I'll be hurting by three.

"I'll be counting the minutes." I murmur, as I turn still grinning like a fool.

I start to walk away taking a few steps then happen to turn my head back, for one last glimpse at her scrumptious back side, before turning the corner that will lead me back to the Shitkick bar. I stop dead in my tracks. The goddess reaches her entire top half of her body straight down through the grave, as though it was an empty box sitting above the ground with no lid. Instead of six foot under with a lid and dirt covering it, and pulls the young man's soul straight out of his body. She turns takes a couple of steps before disappearing. What the hell? It must be some sort of invisible portal, is all I can guess.

I rush back to the spot where she was standing, and try to walk through it the same as she had. I try it twice without finding an opening. I decide she closed the portal behind her. So I give up and start to walk back towards the road when I realize I am not in the same place I was minutes ago. I'm in a different realm all together, an alley lined with gold. I was right it's a portal of some kind. It must be a portal to the heavenly realm where the Gods live.

Becoming a prisoner or one of their slaves does not sound like a fun job to me. Well, I'll be honest with myself, if it was the beautiful soul taker I would be a slave too, I'd rethink the whole scenario. The woman sure is fine and I can't wait to get her alone later tonight.

Honestly I'm not so sure she'll show up, however I sure as hell hope so. If she doesn't, though, I'm in a world of trouble from all four of my brothers not to mention the women folk. Perhaps she was screwing with me making promises she didn't plan to keep in an attempt to get away quicker, with no more questions asked. I'll know the answer soon enough. For now, I'm going to head back to the Shitkick Bar and see if the others came up with any helpful news. I suppose they will be happy about my news of the portals.

11

Staked

Treyvon

Flying on the outskirts of town Brenn and I searched over every last square inch of the Skagit County for hours. We've almost decided to call it quits when we come across the camp where the ritual took place, the gateway to the Cascade Mountains. We see no sign of danger so I fly in landing in close proximity, to what's left of what must be Issy's burnt out bug. Brenn reluctantly waits up in the trees checking them for any sign of these hunters until I'm quite sure it's not a trap. I walk all around using my extra senses and am satisfied no one's been here for a while. The fires are all completely out so I signal for her to come down.

"It's about time," she say's landing with a slight smirk on her face. "I've been taking care of myself all my life Treyvon; did you forget in these few short years since we've met? I think I got sap from those damn pine trees in my hair, not to mention I'm covered in pine needles and spider webs!" she adds a little crossly, shaking her head to get any would be pine needles out of her hair and swatting down her clothes.

I gaze at her porcelain doll like face, milky white soft skin, sea colored blue eyes, long lashes with bow tie shaped lips, still amazed she's mine. Well not officially, but still MINE all the same. I would fight to the death before letting another man take her away from me. She is my Eternalmate even if she will not claim it to be true, nor will she deny.

The woman is relentless she likes to take things slow. Her freedom is too important to her and she doesn't want to give it up quite yet. When I say slow... I mean the slug inching its way across the garden slow. Two years after all is a long time for a vampire to wait for his Eternalmate to agree for it to become official. When I say official, I mean the woman won't even share blood with me. For some damn reason she doesn't want me in her head. She holds the most important part of our bonding in her wee little hands, and if she doesn't commit soon I'm afraid I might kill some poor sucker just for checking her out. I'm still not sure if she doesn't want me in her head because she stores secrets she's not willing to share, or if the truth is she doubts us as a couple?

"What are you gawking at? Is something on my face?" I smile and point towards her nose for the heck of it enjoying her frustration a little because she is so darn cute. She rubs and rubs and I begin to worry she might rub it off so I relent.

"It's gone." I say, with a grin as my lips go to hers. She's startled. She pushes at my chest giggling. I'm not ready to give her lips up quite yet, *she tastes so sweet, and so I hold on tighter and take the kiss deeper.*

"Trey, what are you doing we're here on business not pleasure?"

"There's no one here baby, and you know exactly what I'm doing," I return, with a chuckle slipping my wanting hands around her lushes hips and pulling her closer loving the silky softness of her skin beneath my touch. She calls me her nickname Trey. It's the name I used while helping Maximus bring Carrabella out of her last and final bout of amnesia. She returns the kiss this time pleasing me immensely and I take it deeper, more serious from playful and sweet, to hungry and a hell of a lot more demanding, instantly wanting more...oh so much more, Brenn has a way about her that drives me mad with lust.

I lean her up against a nearby tree trunk reach down and un-snap the button on her short shorts. I try to slide my hand down and inside her little boy cut panties while she pretends to try and fight me off. I groan, loving the softness of her supple skin.

She moans.

Oh yeah...she wants me just as bad. Her hands reach up to my hair brushing her long finger nails through the short length of it. I growl deep in my throat at the ferocity of her touch. My hand reaches up her shirt and I fumble her lovely ripe for the taking breast twisting and teasing. Not enough, my mouth waters and I lust for a sample. I lift up her shirt my lips aiming for her already stiff aroused nipple anxious to place my lips on them...

"Snap! "What the...! It came from behind me close enough I can feel his breath. I peer into Brenn's eyes wide with surprise. I cover her back up pulling her shirt back down over her breasts in one smooth move, whispering in her ear "disappear, and run now..." her eyes show she is not happy with my command, yet follows it all the same. I turn around to the direction the snap had come from keeping my body in front of hers until her presence leaves.

As soon as I turn ready to fight a fist is headed towards my face and even with my speed there is no time to blink besides get out of the way as the blow smashes into my face. His fist like a stone mallet hitting with so much force I see stars right away, crushing my nose to the back of my head. Excruciating pain shoots through my face behind my eyes right on through the back on my head. Run Brenn...! Is the last thing I think, as everything goes black!

12

Running

Brenn

I blast into the night shifting into my raven-self, flying low above the tree lines making it harder for the hunters to follow me if they try. I'm faster than most, but tonight my heart is heavy and my lungs barely hold enough air to keep me up. I am so worried about Trey. I want to charge back into that camp killing the witch hunter. The only reason holding me back is there could be four other hunters with him. It's not like we sensed them or even heard the hunter, not until the snap of the branch directly behind us. Thank the heavens for that Branch!

Trey told me to disappear. To run! So I did, and now I'm headed straight for the Shitkick Bar hoping his clan will still be there waiting for us. I would signal them through the family line, If I could. However, I can't. Only people with shared blood are able to talk to each other telepathically. I am a fool for not sharing blood with Trey. I'm sure he wasn't able to call his brothers before the punch tore through his face rearranging his nose to the back side of his head.

I cringe at the thought tears filling my eyes. It was a terrible sound, bone crushing and he didn't even yell out in pain as he slithered to the ground, but it's a sound I will never forget. My man is so incredibly strong. All I understood was run, run Brenn. I can't talk to him telepathically, yet somehow I can still sense him breathing. He's still alive. I won't accept anything else. I sob. The thought of living without him causes my insides to burn as though I've been drinking acid. The guilt for not agreeing to be his wife would be too much for me. He is my Eternalmate and I was a selfish bitch making him wait. Why was I so cruel?

My reasons appear stupid now. I guess I wanted him to be sure. And to be truthful I like my independents, and love my privacy. I don't want to dictate what he can or can't do and I certainly don't want him to do that to me. I choose not to hear what's in Trey's head. And I prefer my thoughts to be my own. Is that so hard to understand? I don't think so, but Trey on the other hand disagrees.

If he could make me the promise that he would only enter my head if he was worried about me as in, 'there has been no word from me in over ten hours,' saying I'm running late. Then it would be easier for me to consider. I need him to offer me that to be sure his promise would be sincere. After this I don't know what I think. If I had shared blood with Trey I could be speaking with him right now. Tears slip down my eyes as the horror of what might be happening to him enters my mind. Trey is strong a force of nature still the monster blind-sided him and I'm sure it knocked him out.

Almost there - I spot the sign swaying in the air red light flashing - Shitkick bar - OPEN. I flash inside not giving a care of who witnesses me landing in the middle of the room.

I walk over to Buck who points to the back room where Buck and Sophia's small office is located. I appear through the door and when I only spot Marcus, Issy and Sophia, I am alarmed.

"Where are your brothers?" I demand almost out of breath.

Their faces fly to mine.

"What's wrong, where's Treyvon?" Marcus barks, standing up ready for anything, a man always in charge. He instinctively realizes some-things wrong with Trey. The others catching our vibes follow suit under-standing something is not right.

"He was abducted and worse yet he's hurt!" I blurt out with tears stinging the back of my eyes.

"What do you mean? Explain yourself." Asks Maximus forcefully.

"He made me leave him. He wanted me to come and get you." I cry out!

"Hurt! Hurt how?" Carrabella asks forcefully a storm gathering in her sea green eyes.

"Was it the hunters?" Marcus growls.

"Yes, the hunters, well, at least one hunter, I didn't see any others, he creeped up on us so quietly without any warning except a branch snapping."

"How the hell did he sneak up on you? And how did you escape?" Marcus spats with a growl coming from deep inside of his gut.

"Trey shielded me. He told me to run, before he turned around to face the giant." Tears threaten to pour. I must be strong for Treys sake. "As he turned the Hunter smashed him in the face before he could get out of the way, with so much force I swear his nose was rearranged to the back of his head." I sniffle. "I know he's not dead though, he's alive here in my heart." I say, peering into Marcus's furious eyes as I lay my hands across my heart.

"Give me a minute," he barks," I'm trying to message him to find out if he can answer." He doesn't answer. Marcus tries a few more times and somewhere in between trying to get a hold of Trey he messages his brothers about the attack and to get to the Shitkick pronto. He is fuming his face twisted in an angry scowl, his blue eyes hard as steel and his voice deadly. There's no doubt they will save Trey or die trying.

It only took a few more minutes for all three brothers to appear. "Where is he?" Maximus spats barely consuming his anger.

"The same spot Issy and I were last night. The spot where her car broke down."

"I'm going to kill the hunter who did that to Trey!" Maximus spats, then leans over and kisses his Carrabella, "Keep safe baby, there is always the chance this is a trap leading us away from our ladies. Call me at any threat. Do you understand me? Any threat at all. Our baby boy is going to want his mommy back when we return home." he says, with such love and sweetness it almost makes me jealous. And the way they gaze at each other after five hundred centuries most people only dream of. My eyes go to Carrabella's.

She rolls her eyes at Maximus, "I always do," she answers him half smiling, but her green sea colored eyes show turmoil. "I would ask if we could come, but the answer is in your eyes love. Hurry, go save Treyvon and bring him back to us!" She demands forcefully, pushing him towards the door.

"You bet your sweet little ass we will," says Anthony, causing Maximus to punch him on the shoulder.

"Hey, keep it clean when talking to my woman," Maximus growls.

"Sorry, I wasn't thinking," he spats, putting his palms up in surrender. "I'm beside myself pissed those monsters attacked Treyvon, and I don't even want to think about what else they could be doing to him."

Carrabella nods, "Its ok, I understand - now go!" she answers, while pushing him towards the door too.

"Any of you been able to reach him?" inquires Anthony. All the brothers shake their heads back and forth as in no!

"Let's ride," Marcus growls! His eyes flash to Issy's before glancing away with so much speed I barely caught it. "Don't any of you women even think about leaving these premises until we return." He speaks in a voice so icy and deep it gives me the creeps. No one say's a word. "Am I understood?" he demands, in the same icy deep tone.

"Yes." We all say in unison with shaky voices. Maximus temper is quick, but it strikes like lightening and it is gone. To everyone except his Carrabella, Marcus on the other hands temper is different altogether he is not someone you want to reckon with. His temper is chilling, as in - bone chilling. His voice alone is enough to freeze a person's blood right where they stand. The truth is Marcus has never lost his temper in front of me, yet it is enough to witness him like this; to understand you never want to be around him completely out of control.

"Let me help!" demands Issy, taking a step forward.

Again his eyes fly to Issy's. "No, I need you safe." He retorts, sternly as if talking to a child, before clearing his throat. Her eyebrows go up and her mouth flies open wide as she stares at him in a way I can only describe as disbelief. Marcus turns on his heels and heads out the back door to the office with his brothers in tow. Hmm, I wonder what all that's about as my mind skips back to Trey. Oh baby I pray you're still alive. Hold strong - help is on the way!

I gape out the window as the brothers one by one shift into their eagle forms and fly into the air at a speed I'm sure is not recommended wishing I was going with them to help. I flop to the small couch alongside the wall and bawl my eyes out not caring that I look like a complete baby, while the others try to comfort me.

"It will be ok. They will save him. There is no doubt about it." comforts Carrabella, my dearest friend as she puts her arms around my shoulders rocking me like a mother cuddles her child.

I acknowledge other words of comfort from Buck and Sophia as Buck leans down and says, "Here drink this," as he hands me a shot of something or other.

I peek up as Sophia shakes her head up and down, "Go ahead dear, take a drink, it will calm your nerves."

My eyes stray to Issy who is sitting in the corner with her head down saying nothing at all. This worries me even more. She of all people has first-hand knowledge of what these hunters are capable of.

I take the shot. I cringe. I lay my head back on the couch.

"What if he is dead?" I say out loud to no one in particular.

"He's not." they all proclaim like a chorus of a song.

"You don't know that. What if I left him alone to fight those monsters instead of staying and fighting beside him like an Eternalmate should do?" I ask mostly talking to myself.

"Maximus could feel his heart beating. He told me himself." says Carrabella in a calming tone. I squint to peer up at her.

"Is that the truth? He told you that?" I ask her.

"No. I read it from his mind. Remember we share the Eternalmate line. I can hear anything he thinks if I want to." she says cautiously.

"I understand your point, it's loud and clear. Do you consider I haven't been thinking the same thing over and over again in my head

Carra? If I'd only shared blood with Trey I could be speaking with him right now. You don't need to tell me what a fool I've been," I say punching my own chest, "I've been chastising myself this whole time."

"I did not mean..."

"Oh yes you did Carra, even if you didn't mean to imply it out loud. And you're painfully correct." I say, sitting down planting my hands to my face bending my head and sobbing.

"Now, now ladies this isn't helping. Let's make ourselves useful instead." comforts Sophia, picking up her IPad.

"Yes, you're right Sophia, but first I'm going to get everyone a strong drink on the house. I think we all could use one."

"Great Idea Buck." says Carra, rubbing my back always the good friend and I instantly feel bad for scolding her. I'm such a bitch sometimes.

"I wonder if I had stayed and fought by his side if I would have been any help."

"Probably not, Treyvon told you to run. Don't you see, he wanted you to get back up? You did the best thing possible running here to get his brothers. Neither of you stood a chance against those hunters." says Issy, finally breaking her quiet treatment.

"What's that supposed to mean...?" asks Carrabella, chin raised proudly, hands flying to her hips.

"I don't mean any disrespect, but these hunters can't be stopped. That's why I've been on the run my whole life." adds Issy sitting her forehead back down on her knees.

"Oh you poor dear." says Sophia, in her normal comforting tone.

"Please don't have pity on me. This is my way of life, it's the way it's always been, so it's no big deal." Answers Issy, and I can tell how proud she is and how hard her life has been, causing a piece of the wall I've inadvertently built between us, to chip away. I cry and I cry until there are no more tears inside of me. I get up and walk into the bathroom and barely make it to the stool, before wrenching my gut out. When done I walk to the sink. Turn the water on and wash my face and rinse my mouth out. I stare into the mirror. 'You are done crying now,' I say using voice control, 'Trey is going to be all right.' I leave the bathroom walk back to the office get on my cell and start Face booking and emailing everyone on my friend list about these hunters. The same as the rest of the group are doing.

Hours later I am going stir crazy with worry. Not one word from any of the men to fill us in on what's happening and I can tell the others concern has grown to high alert, too. I'm about to take off headed back to where Trey was when Carrabella startles me.

"He's been found," Carrabella jumps up from her seat looking at me, "he's hurt, but alive with no life threatening injuries, and there is no sign left of the hunters." She say's, telling us exactly what Maximus is saying in her mind, and all of us cry happy joyful tears. And again I am jealous and angry because I cannot talk to Trey myself.

"Tell them to be watchful, because there was no sign of the hunters before either. They could be in the area hiding waiting to pounce." I say, skeptical even through my happy thankful tears. He's alive. Trey is alive.

13

Saved

Treyvon

I hear them yelling in my head, my brothers all four. Over and over
again their words keep chanting.

"Treyvon wake up!" It's Marcus barking at me.

"Treyvon we're coming for you?" Anthony sounds alarmed.

"Damn it Treyvon, quit goofing around and wake your ass up!" coming from my twin Maximus, of course. I shake my head enjoying my
slumber not wanting to wake up. They are relentless chanting in my head
messing with my sleep until finally I've had enough and am Livid when
I shout into their ears, "Shut the hell up. I'm awake already! What the
hell is wrong with all of you?" I demand into their bullheads with all the
power I can muster so much it echoes through my own head causing me
to stir and wake up for real.

Then as my head clears and I am more awake, I'm not sure what over-
takes my senses first the smoke surrounding me and filling my lungs,
the heat, as though I'm being cooked alive - or the fact I am naked arms
spread eagle while my feet are bound together straight down as though
I'm staked to a cross. I know it's true before I even open my eyes. It's

become painfully obvious why my brothers were trying to wake me and the pain and embarrassment of the witch hunter sneaking up on us when I was in the midst of making love to Brenn, comes back to me in full force. Damn, if I get out of this mess she will probably never forgive me.

But that's not important right now...I am desperate to see if Brenn escaped. It's not like I could call for her as she hasn't shared blood with me yet, damn her stubbornness! I try to open my eyes again and force them to peer all around which is difficult with the burning so I blink to clear my vision. From where I can see she is nowhere to be seen. I try to call out her name, but it comes out raspy and barely audible. I can only presume if they had captured her she would be staked here beside me. So my hope is she's made it to safety and that's why my brothers were calling me sounding worried. That's all I care about is Brenn's safety. I'll never forget the surprise on her shocked face as I ordered her to run! But of course she's made it. The reason why my brothers were so determined to wake me. She saw me get knocked out as she fled. Damn it's not something a man wants his woman to witness.

The smoke is thick and hard to see through even with my special site. I don't think they are trying to start me on fire, or if they are they did a damn poor job of it. Hell it's all guesswork. My only thought is how were they able to sneak up on us? Yes, I realize I was distracted or a better word is consumed by Brenn and where my lips were headed. Her hot little body is all that I could think of, but still it's not like me or her not to be aware of our surroundings. I didn't sense them and I was told the scent would alert us miles before they could get anywhere near us.

"Yes, she's safe. Hold strong!" Maximus confirms.

"We're almost there." Say's Marcus determination in his voice. "Stay awake!" he demands.

"Hiking in." says Anthony. "Count to twenty."

"I saw what the hunter's did to you." Says James.

"The fuckers are dead!" growls Maximus. "Tell them to prepare for hell!"

For the first time in my life the sound of my brothers voices are better than the angels singing to my ears.

I don't see a point to use energy to message them back; instead I take Anthony's advice and start to count to twenty while trying to peer around me.

Nineteen. It's come to my attention that nobody else seems to be here.

Eighteen. Not one hunter.

Seventeen. Nor any voices.

Sixteen. Nothing, but the sound of this fire crackling beneath me.

Fifteen. This is odd.

Fourteen. The pain of the ropes cutting into my hands and feet is almost unbearable, please tell me you didn't bring the women folk to witness this.

Thirteen.

Twelve. Can't see anything.

Eleven.

Ten. Hurry the hell up.

Nine. I'd like to warn them of whose here.

Eight.

Seven. My head is spinning.

Six. I try again. "Whose there? What do you want with me?"

five.

Four. Feet burning now,

Three. "Show yourselves,"

Two. Shit! "It's a trap!"

I send a quick all out message as I see Maximus and Marcus coming through the trees in front of me swords held high. I gasp - my eyes search the trees and all around as my hands try to rip the knots off my swollen wrists expecting the witch hunters to blindside them at any time the way they had done Brenn and I earlier.

Maximus appears next to me slashing the binds and taking my sore muscled body down from the cross like stake, trying to help me stand. My feet are slightly burned and it hurts like hell. I need blood now. It's the only thing besides going to ground that will heal me. All the while Marcus is standing guard. Maximus rolls up his sleeve, "take what is offered!" he says between clenched teeth, obviously seething wanting to kill the bastards that did this to me.

"Not now," I growl. "Go find them. Their hidden, but I bet they're here somewhere. This is what they did earlier when Issy and I arrived. I used my powers to scope the area out from the ground while Issy used hers to check out the trees. There was no sign of anything evil or not evil it was as if no one had ever been here before. Not even you and Issy."

"Take what is offered," he demanded as though I hadn't said anything, his eyes menacing small and crazy looking the way he gets before he usually loses it.

"Asshole," I say grabbing his wrist and biting down, but so thankful at the same time. Maximus my twin his blood is the strongest blood I could drink right now. I feel its healing powers quickly and the powerful rich flavor makes me stand stronger even with burnt feet. Thanks to my twins blood they'll be fine within a few hours as though it never had happened. One of the good quirks of being a vampire, I think somberly.

I am glad my brothers are here but anxious at the same time wondering where the hell these hunters are hidden. Like us they are able to disappear without a trace. Even with our super human sense of smell you can't detect them until they're upon you. The more important thought is why we can't sense them. We're Vampire even if we take the blood pill we still hold seventy percent of our powers and for some of us who are always working them, honing them, we are closer to eighty five or ninety so we can take the pill without it being any real risk. All five of us brothers take after our father and were already twice as big as an even stronger than most men, or children at the time when are village was attacked and we were turned so many centuries ago. That being said so afterwards we were even stronger faster and had better sense altogether than most. My senses never let me down before. We should still be able to sense all evil. I release his wrist noticing his skin turning a little pale. Shit, he's let me take too much.

"Damn it Maximus why didn't you stop me?" I hiss at him.

He shrugs. "I don't know what you're talking about. You needed the blood I gave it freely. So your welcome asshole." He says quietly before turning and walking away. I could tell by the intensity in his dark eyes that the wheels were already turning, though.

"You've been drinking a little too much Homebrew," I whisper grinning, a hell of a lot better thanks to Maximus. I shift into my eagle form not wanting to stand on my feet while they are healing yet determined to do more investigating around me. I hear him chuckle as I fly into the trees.

"It's about time you covered yourself, I was a little tired of looking at your skinny naked ass." He says still laughing.

"I felt them the other night, but I don't now. I think their gone." Marcus cuts into our conversation.

"Me either, but that's the point it's eerie in the way that it doesn't appear like anyone's been here besides you and Brenn today. I see no signs besides Issy's car, the fire, and the stake you were hanging on that anyone else has been here at all. Nothing. No lingering scents, no foot prints, no hand prints, and no broken twigs - nothing." It's like you punched yourself in the face knocking yourself out. Woke up, built a cross and staked it into the ground. Built a fire underneath it and then climbed up on it tying you to the stake. The facts are eerie to say the least. What the hell is going on here?" Maximus grumbles, stumped!

"I told you. This is exactly as it was before." I say.

James and Anthony enter from the other side of the hill out of breath. I was beginning to wonder why they hadn't shown their faces yet.

14

The Shitkick Bar

Marcus

Flying into the outskirts of town we shift back into our human forms. Making ourselves appear decent as we walk towards the bar. James is acting a little anxious and I wonder if he's expecting trouble here in town. I walk a little slower and say into James head discretely, "What's up...you expecting trouble?"

He peers up at me oddly, shaken even and then shakes his head back and forth. "Did you for see something you need to tell me?"

He nods a 'no' gesture once again still acting oddly. Hmm, what the hell's wrong with him? I wonder.

"Did you find anything out at the grave yard today?" I ask verbally this time presuming whatever it is spooked him. He stops in his tracks. I stop too. The others keep walking in a mad rush towards the bar anxious to get to their woman I suppose, Treyvon needs to go to ground and get extra healing, yet probably won't until we've avenged him and Brenn.

"Yes. I met the receiving angel, Mariah. Marcus you wouldn't believe it unless you behold her with your own eyes. The woman is more than stunning. She's an aphrodisiac, the sexiest woman this side of heaven."

He says starry eyed which quickly turns to agitated causing me to wonder if he hadn't planned on sharing this information with me, yet once I asked couldn't contain it any longer. Ahh, another fallen angel as it were, the boy's got it bad, almost as bad as me I fear.

"Really...?" I grin. "I had heard that before about her. Did she give you any answers? Or agree to talk to the god of light?" I ask hopeful, yet at the same time still not comfortable with dealing with this angel to get to the Gods.

"No... well... Yes. What I mean is I am meeting her later tonight after she gets off of work and she stated she'll answer them then. Of course, she could have been screwing with me and not plan on showing at all, I guess only time will tell." He murmurs. Yes, indeed I read an article about this beautiful gold covered vixen. It claimed she's sharp and talented at getting what she wants. My sneaking suspicion is this time she wants my brother.

"Well, let's hope she shows." I say with a sly grin. "What times your date?" I clear my throat, "I mean your inquisition?" I add hoping there's time for a quick meeting and some nourishment beforehand. I need to get a run down on what everyone found out today and talk more about changing plan B & C. Plan A is already screwed.

"Three a.m., so about two hours." He says reading what was on my mind.

A couple of seconds later we walk into the bar and I am relieved to feel the air conditioning. Today it's about thirty degrees cooler than yesterday, still well above the normal seventy. A hundred and twenty yesterday was a record high. I see my clan over at a large corner table and turn that way. Everyone else in our clan is already here seated and ordering.

"What will it be Marcus, whiskey or beer?" asks Sophia looking overly tired.

"Whiskey, but I'll get it. Take a load off, Sophia." I say trying to save her a little work heading towards the bar.

"But..." I hear her protest as I keep walking grabbing a bottle of whiskey and a glass as I go. I see Bucks in the kitchen cooking so I walk over to ask him to come join us, when he's able. "Need any help?" I ask. Assuming he'd decline. He doesn't like anyone doing the cooking, but him. He is real proud of his cooking and says that's why people keep coming back. I would never mention that it's probably the fact that there's nowhere else in town like this to eat, that keeps them coming back. Why bother, it makes him happy.

"Nah...I'm almost done. Need anything to eat... a steak?"

"Nah, I think I'm good. One hell of a night though. How's it going at the Concrete High School, everyone behaving?"

"Yep, all's quiet from what I'm told. Bringing in the reserves to watch over them was a real good idea."

"I'm glad it worked out and they were willing to help."

"Trey looks a little worse for wear, but I reckon he'll be fine within a few hours. I got to admit I'm a little confused on what I was told. Why would they kidnap Treyvon, hang him on a stake only to abandon him for you easily to retrieve? Was there any sign of the hunters?"

"Nope, eerily enough there was no sign whatsoever, and the same question has been gnawing at us all. The only thing that comes to mind is they were aware of us coming and fled before we arrived. For all I know they didn't plan to kidnap Treyvon in the first place. They seem to like to play games to put fear in to people. The other night they performed a ritual of burning Issy's car and had voodoo dolls hung on stakes that looked like her clan."

"Hmm, could be, but it's still hard to believe they were able to hide from Treyvon and Issy earlier after what you said about them, their size, and the raunchy odor. I don't like the idea of them being able to hide so easily especially from a vampire. I never even knew it was possible to hide ones scent from us."

"That makes two of us. They're a puzzle and we need to figure out all the pieces before we can stop them. What powers they possess for one and how to kill them for the other."

"Speaking of puzzles, I'm curious of why Issy, doesn't possess more information on these hunters. She stated she's been running from them all her life?"

"Ya got me. She also stated she's tried to kill them, on the other hand there hasn't been any time for her to elaborate. She says she runs they follow and that's been her life. The truth is I believe her. She's terrified of them after what they did to her kin."

"Hmm, well let's hope we come up with better information on how to stop them, before it's too late."

"I'll second that motion. It's quiet though. Much too quiet and all I can say is no one should be going anywhere without an escort, especially the women."

"I'll pass the word along to anyone stupid enough to be wandering out tonight. As for Sophia, she won't be leaving the premises."

"Good. You know what Buck; I think I will take a steak - rare. When you're done cooking why don't you come sit with us?" I say realizing he'd come either way. I walk back over to the corner table. I don't even need to turn my head to sense where Issy is sitting. I knew it the minute I walked into the room even though her seat is in the far corner hidden from everyone except for the people sitting at this table's sight. She doesn't turn my way which is a huge let down after this long hard day. I was hoping she would be a little concerned about me. Why doesn't she understand I want her safe? Her menu slides down a smidgen and her eyes snap to mine. I hear the word 'safe' echo from her mind to mine and back and I'm not sure if she caused it to happen or did I?

I nod.

She moves the menu back up to hide her eyes. Her hand trembles slightly showing me how this is affecting her. She needs to be safe. I shake off the urge to go to her. I want to hold her. I need to show her that I will always keep her safe. I realize this is not the time to comfort her; I will enjoy doing that later. I need to prove my worth to her. Any fool knows words mean nothing without action and I am definitely a man of action.

I sit down at the only chair left at the table and it happens to be directly across from Issy. My suspicion is that the family planned it this way, then again its fine with me. Eventually she will put the menu down and face me. I smile.

A moment later Buck comes with three steaks one for Maximus, him and I, placing them before us. Scanning around the table I am assured the rest are eating their food already. Well, that is except for Issy whom obviously hasn't decided what she wants, or a stab in the dark it's her lack of money. I announce to Buck, "The meals for everyone at this table for the duration of their visit is on me, Buck, their money is worthless here."

Buck shakes his head. My brother's hooted and holler. Their wives thank me, however Issy doesn't say a thing.

On the other hand the menu could be in her hands to hide herself from me. Buck pulls up a chair from another table, sits down and we all eat talking lightly and having a few drinks. When were done eating we officially start the meeting.

James goes first excited to share with us the news of the portals. For some reason he doesn't share with the rest of them about the receiving angels' beauty, or his date. Nor the fact that he hasn't gotten any answers from her yet. He's probably afraid Maximus might grab her by her wings, until he gets answers which wouldn't surprise me one bit. Or Anthony might try to steal her with his intellect. I can tell he's getting antsy and wants this meeting to be over before she appears.

Next shares Anthony telling everyone about the blog he started and explaining to all the rest of us who are not so savvy with electronics, how to use it. Thousands of people visited it he says.

Next Sophia and Buck tell the group about Facebook and all the shares so far. And how that it is all anyone is talking about on Facebook, and twitter even though a lot of people think it's a joke.

"Who the hell are these guys and how do we stop them?" Marcus barks, bringing me out of my day dreaming.

"My thoughts exactly." I say, shaking my head back and forth as my eyes stray to Issy, who now lowered her menu to the table. Her eyes are clouded.

"From what I can tell this is over every form of media known to man, yet so far no one's seen or heard of them, anywhere. People are starting to doubt us thinking this is a big practical joke. A ruse if you will." Remarks

Anthony, frowning as he pours a shot of the whiskey I had brought to the table, then downs it.

"All I can say is we," Treyvon holds up his hand threaded with Brenn's, "saw exactly how real they are. We've had first-hand meetings with at least one of them. He snuck up on us, two Va'atacos, as you all understand that's not an easy task. He smashed me in the face so hard that it knocked me out long enough for him to practically crucify me, while burning me alive. Did you put that on your Facebook?" Treyvon demands. "No one's seen or heard of them my ass." Treyvon signals for the whiskey and Anthony sends it flying across the table.

"Yeah, what about Issy's car and the five burning stakes, with effigies burning on them, did you tell Facebook about that?" Carrabella adds, rolling her eyes.

"They're obviously real and here example one, Treyvon's face. Perhaps we should snap a shot and put that on Facebook, Twitter, Pinterest, and Instagram. They're just good at hiding. My opinion is and I would bet money the ability to mask themselves is one of their gifted powers. They are able to completely blend into their environment, and hide their scent from immortals." Adds Brenn, "Because that's sure as hell what they did to us."

"I've experienced these same things for a century. Nobody ever believed me until Marcus." Issy says, peering up at me before quickly glancing away. My chest burns and the heat is so hot it spreads through every cell.

We go on and on saying the same damn things not getting anywhere finishing the entire bottle of whiskey, and a second one to boot. All of it only guesses and speculation. I had expected more.

All I can hope for is that this 'Mariah,' James is meeting, can help. We decide to go home and try to do some more research from there and basically wait till somebody messages us. There is nothing else we can do at this point.

James sent out word in his magical dream world that seems to form in his head. And Anthony sent out emails and texts to trusted sorcerers and witch friends around the world hoping they can enlighten us on the magic part of all of this. It's just a little trickery with a witch, a demi-god, a vampire, and that's not counting the so called Christian witch hunters. What a mess, I think again.

I send everyone home including Issy; well basically I ignored her the rest of the night just as she was ignoring me. Persuading myself that it was better this way even though I was sure deep down it wasn't true. Even with all that is going on my mind and body is hyper aware of hers.

As everybody left in our group I held back talking to Buck in his office, stalling because I wanted to get a gander at James receiving angel Mariah, before I leave. I'm a little skeptical about her and want to make sure it's not some kind of trap for him. For all I know it was a witch hunter masked as this beautiful receiving angel.

It's not like they let themselves be seen every day. And further more why did this so called receiving angel think we were here to save the witch hunters, instead of killing them. It all sounds a little fishy to me and I already wish I hadn't agreed to let him investigate further into her story about the Gods. My gut sizzles at the thought of any of this coming back down and hurting Issy. Issy's name is not supposed to be brought up in the conversation only the fact of the cursed hunters, which they already seem to understand more about them then they're letting on, if we give out any information at all to them. Either the woman is a fraud or she knows exactly what's going on around here.

15

Date

James

$\mathcal{I}$ glance at the time on my cell, three ten. I take another shot and enjoy the hearty warm flavor swishing it around in my mouth before swallowing, while wondering if this angel was ever on time? Or perchance my speculations come to light, and she never planned to come at all? Perhaps she was just placating me with all her sexy flirtations. I don't think my body could handle that. Just thinking about Mariah's lushes' curves made me hard and it hasn't changed all day. Even with the crazy day we had with Treyvon being kidnapped and all.

I'll give her the benefit of a doubt and wait a half hour more, not one minute later. Besides, to be completely fair her work could be keeping her later than expected. I wonder how many souls she collects in a night. It could be one or it could be in the hundreds or more, who's to say. I think it must be a lonely sad job though, especially for a woman like her to perform each night all alone. For me just standing there waiting for her in the grave yard tonight by that young boy's soul, depressed the hell out of me. What it must be like every single night of the week to hear all those souls calling out to you, knowing each and every ones sad stories. Or possibly happy stories too. But I don't imagine that not too many people are ever happy to die.

I glance at my phone again. Ten more minutes that's all I'll give her. I order another drink from Buck noticing that Marcus is still here too. Why didn't he go home with Issy? They seem to have something pretty strong going on between them. I drum my fingers on the table, thinking about all of today's strange events.

"Hello, sorry I'm late." She apologizes, first thing. "Did I keep you waiting too long?" she asks, before flashing her eyes down at her cell screen. She appears nervous, wide eyed, skin pink, breathing off a bit.

Whoa. I take one glimpse of her and all is forgiven, though. Holy shit she's hot!

"No. Not long." I lie. Grateful she's standing before me. "Your beauty is beyond compare."

"You flatter Me." she takes a quick glance down at her self-twirling around for me to admire all sides and boy howdy does she carry one sweet ass, "it's nothing. I always dress like this." She uses her hand as a fan as if she's hot even though Buck keeps the air conditioning on high. She talks like she's terribly conceded, although I suspect that isn't the case. I think where she comes from they probably enforce rules about stating the truth at all times, being angels and all, and don't see anything wrong with it. I love it. The honesty - It's sexy as hell. Imagine a woman who honestly accepts who she is and doesn't complain about herself. What's not to like. I grin.

"Take a seat." I say getting up and pulling out her chair, surprising her.

"Oh, thank you." She grins. "I can't stay long, so let's get to this." She says, quietly conspiratorially leaning her head across the table towards mine. "What are your questions?"

"What's the rush?"

"I'm only allowed to be here from midnight until dawn." She whispers looking around to confirm there's no one hidden in the corners listening to us. There were a lot of poor souls tonight. Sorry, I worked as fast as I could to get here sooner."

"Oh!" I say glancing out the window, then at my cell, three forty-five. "Not much time. Only a couple of hours left. Do you want to go somewhere more private?" I ask hoping like hell she answers yes. There is a small inn down the road I could take her to. It's the only one in town that I know of. I want nothing more than to get this woman alone and her clothes off. The questions can wait, till later.

She shakes her head up and down. "Yes. Please."

Five minutes later we walk outside the door of the bar and after taking a couple of steps we appear in a room of gold. What the hell! I'm startled at first...and then I see the king size bed sitting in the middle of the room and I automatically relax, grinning. She's brought me to her realm and more importantly, her room which is also covered in gold.

She glances up at me shyly putting her index finger upon her lips. Boy do I want those delicious looking lips. "You like?"

"Yes...Yes I do." I reply as I take her in my arms kissing her. Whoa...I feel the jolt immediately. Her lips so soft so sweet, the flavor of honey mixed with cotton candy, oddly enough, but sweet, so unbelievably sweet, I want to lick them whole. What a treat, a yummy delight. Little electric pulses send shivers down my spine and straight to my groin. I harden immediately. I can tell she felt it too. I stop kissing her for a moment and we gaze into each other's eyes, already turning different shades, ready for the love making to come. Are hearts beat as one touched by each other's passion and we've barely begun. I go to kiss her again...longing for more of her taste.

James, where the hell are you? Marcus demands in my head startling me.

What the hell? I pull back away from her surprise in my eyes. How the hell did Marcus reach me from another realm?

"What is it, what's wrong?" she says looking alarmed. "Is my breath yucky, should I get a mint? Don't you want me?" her voice asks in a whisper, hurt as she puts her hand out blowing into it and then tries to take-in her - own breath. It was all I could do not to laugh.

"Hell yes I want you, I'd be a fool not to." I hurriedly answer not wanting her to think this is about her.

"Oh. I see. You want your part of the favor first?"

Oh shit. In my haste to get her clothes off I had forgotten all about the questions it's imperative that I ask her.

"Well there is that, although that's not why I stopped. Could you give me a moment? By the way Mariah, this has nothing to do with you, and everything to do with my big brother talking in my head!"

"Huh?" She asks looking even more confused than before. Wording the words with her lips, "your brother?"

I nod.

Marcus what the hell were you doing following me?

I had a suspicion; she might not be what she seems. She agreed to meet you a little too quickly for me, causing me to wonder why she let you see her in the first place. They are only seen if they want to be. Besides, you said you were meeting with her here at the Shitkick. Where are you now?

It's none of your damn business, but I'm in her realm if you really must be enlightened. Ps Maximus, I don't need a baby sitter.

What?

You heard me. I say noticing Mariah is pacing around the room. Shit her time is limited. I need to get Marcus out of my head.

Get the hell out of there now you idiot, before the Gods realize you're there! Don't you realize this could be a trap? You could become their slave.

Okay, okay, hold your horses. Once I'm done with what I came here to do I'll get out. I say, not planning to budge an inch until I'm done doing what we came here to do, yet wanting to placate him until then. I can't concentrate with him in my head. But the fact is if I shut him out he will kick my ass when I get back, well anyways he'll try and we'll both be a bloody mess.

Good, now hurry it up. And by the way don't think for one single minute that the heavenly realm you're in could save you from me, if you don't follow my orders! He growls, with such force it hurt my ear drum. Jerk!

An hour is all I ask for. Now please shut up. I swear the tingling on the back on my neck is caused by the menacing grin I bet he's wearing right now.

One hour is all you get. So hurry the hell up!

I stand and walk over to her trying to shake that conversation from my head so I can just concentrate on her, "now where were we," I purr taking her in my arms. She stiffens. Not good.

"I thought you wanted to take care of business first," she snaps, flashing daggers at me. I've hurt her feelings.

"Hmm, if you wish, but isn't this part of the business?" I whisper near her ear noticing her breath catch as I take a nibble.

"Let's do this right. Fair is fair. What are your questions?" she asks all professional bringing me to sit at her small table.

"Okay, if that's how you want it, I'd be happy to oblige." I say surprised at the deepness of my own voice.

"It's the way it needs to be, your questions first, then umm...you know... umm other things." she chirps shyly. While my cock on the other hand is so hard it's beginning to be painful.

"If you say so, woman, let's get this over with and out of the way. Do you know of a God by the name of Celeste - the God of light I'm told?"

"Yes. There are many Gods, nevertheless I recall a bad story surrounding her."

"That is what my source says too. Can you tell me your version?"

"Yes, it was a big deal and was talked about for decades. The rumors were so bad that her family was shunned for quite a few years. If I'm correct it had to do with her mortal husband. The story goes that he tricked her into marrying him just to steal her powers, however her father got word of his plan and kicked him out of the realm never to return. It is said they had a daughter named Meredith who they haven't been able to locate for a decade, she's presumed dead. It is said that Celeste and her father quit speaking after that. Why do you ask of them?" she inquires eyeing me suspiciously.

"I'll get to that later. I was told Meredith and her mother Celeste had a bad relationship? Is that true?" hmm, so they don't realize she's dead.

"That's an odd question, but I've been told they were always at odds. Meredith blamed her mother for not protecting her father. She even believed her mom had a part in his death. It's said she despised her. Why are you so interested in Celeste?" she asks, twining her finger around one of the curls cupping her face.

"I might need her to help us break a curse. Could you procure me a meeting with her?"

She gasps. "In the name of our father - please don't ask me to do this." She lays her hand on her chest.

"Why?" I ask frustrated. All I want to do right now is get her naked and instead it's imperative to talk business. The clock is ticking and Marcus will expect me back within the hour.

"More than likely it's a sore subject to her. And my guess is she probably doesn't like to talk about it with her closest family or friends, besides an angel whom she cares nothing about. It could make her furious and she might damn me straight to hell." She says, shivering wrapping her arms around each other.

I laugh. "I doubt that would happen, but if your chicken that's ok. I wouldn't want anything to happen to you."

"Cha... chicken! Did you just call me a chicken?" she stands straight up putting her hands on her sweet lushes hips, oh man hips that I want more than anything to be slamming into right now. Even so I can't help, but admire her stubborn side. "I'm no chicken! I'm a smart woman who doesn't want the God's mad at me. Some of those Gods can be ruthless. They play with us as though we were toys. We are their slaves, nothing more. Granted they also spoil us and give us anything we want. But if we cross them all bets are off."

"I see." I say cracking my knuckles. "I can't ask you to do anything that could put you in harm's way. We'll come up with a different idea. Thank you for your time though." I say, getting up.

"Wait!" she say's putting her hand in the air. Perhaps there is another way. My friend Caroline happens to be the daughter of one of Celeste's friends, the God of trials. I could sway her into seeing what she could find out for us. I'll invite her out for lunch and drinks tomorrow and talk her into it then. It could work...!" She smiles brightly, "Couldn't it? But first before I use my friend and put myself on the line for you, I need to understand why this is so important to you?"

I nod. Now we're getting somewhere. I share with her all that's happened in the last few days, as quickly as I am able. Explaining that no one is really safe from the witch hunters and she agrees to help.

"Are there any more questions?" she asks with a sexy smile, and then licks her sweet hot lips.

"Just one."

"Okay, what is it?"

"Why did you think I was here to free the hunters?"

"Silly man, I'm an angel my mind is over filling with peoples secrets. Now, I want my part of the bargain." She purrs pouty lips shaped into a kiss.

"Come here." I say, realizing she's changing the subject. I'll let it lie for now.

She shakes her head 'no.' And I am let down. No, did she say no? My mind tries to comprehend that while my body is demanding what was promised. A growl escapes me before I can stop it.

"Not so fast," she says. Looking me up and down like I'm a fruity Popsicle she wants to lick, and as if on cue I feel my dick busting out the seams of my jeans.

"Make up your mind, woman." I purr.

"Take off your shirt," she orders as she begins to un-zip her own and lifts it up over her head careful, not to mess up her perfect golden hair. I follow suit and immediately shed mine. She is beautiful. Soft gold dusted skin. High firm, full weighty-breasts, with a waist so small I could put my hands around it. 'Barbie' might have some competition here. She peers through eyes that want to devour me, and I'd be more than happy to participate. I am so caught up in this angel; I just can't believe my luck this day.

"Sit!" she orders. I sit on her bed, getting hotter by the moment from this seduction she's carrying out.

"Don't touch me." She warns, eyebrow in the air as she saunters towards me stopping between my legs. She goes down to her knees. My mouth is instantly dry. I've died and went to heaven is all I can think. I groan, wetting my lips. She chuckles, and it's a deep rich sound. She reaches out and pulls my boots off one by one, much to my amazement. I can't remember a woman ever doing that to me before. Once she's taken my socks off too she tells me to stand.

Once I stand up she orders," take your pants off." as she reaches for my buckle on my belt and then unsnaps my jeans. As I pull them down I see her stand reach for her back zipper and slowly pulls it down inch by slow inch like a dance causing my mouth to water. Holy mother of....this woman is sizzling hot and I want nothing more than to grab a hold of her, lifting her up with her legs straddling my waist her back against the wall and take her hard and fast the rest of the night. Oh I want it slow too...but right now I want it hard hot and fast after her making me wait all day long. As if reading my mind she walks over to the wall sliding her back against the coolness of it. She smiles and says, "well come on then. I want it the same way." Then she dips one of her hands in her bra massaging her nipple. I groan.

Whoa...how does she do that? Did I speak out loud or did she read my mind? It doesn't matter right now I sprint to her in two giant steps stripping her of her bra and her panties so fast she didn't even realize they were gone as I raise her up and she slips her legs around my waist.

Our mouths are going crazy on each other sucking, biting, nibbling, tongues entangling slipping into each other's throats, licking, practically eating each other alive. I reach my hand down between her strong, but soft legs to see if she is anywhere near as ready for me as I am ready for her. And I am pleasantly surprised to find she is slippery wet and her membranes are swelling begging for release she wants me so bad. I stick my fingers in my mouth as her eyes peer at me mesmerized. "Umm sweet as peaches," I say enjoying the way it raises her heart rate and causes her breath to catch. I lick off every drop never taking my eyes off hers. I can't hold back any longer I need her now, I've wanted her since the minute I laid eyes on her a few agonizing hours ago. But first I need to make her scream for it.

I lift her further up the wall on to my shoulders with her legs hanging over my shoulders down my back and go to work. It doesn't take too long before she is begging and I love the sound. "Please Please James."

"Are you sure about this?" I whisper, between licks giving her one last chance to change her mind as I slide her down my body agonizingly slow. "I can't wait much longer to be inside you. It's going to be a wild ride, but I promise next time it'll be agonizingly slow."

"Yes, oh please. More than I've ever been sure about anything. Please...Please James and I want it fast and hard...too."

All I can think is this woman is awesome, as I enter her quickly, slamming myself in to her all the way to the hilt. I give her a moment to adjust and then do it again over and over, again and again rising higher each time. Fast then slow, fast then slow, as deep as I can go. She screams with delight. Moaning, and calling out my name, scratching my back with her long golden tipped finger nails. This succeeds in turning me on more with every scratch, and every moan. I want to give her more and more of me, and all the pleasure I can bestow on her. And I swear our minds are synced as one, because we simply know what each other want and needs.

She matches me hit for hit with so much strength I am simply amazed at her vitality. She squeals, harder James harder! Oh yeah... touch me ...oh yeah ...right there...oh oh ...don't move...oh yeah...oooh yes ...right there... oh yeah. This goddess knows what she wants sexually and I revel in it. We fall to the floor slick with sweat rolling around on the floor and I turn her over slapping her butt hard and she likes it just like I thought she would. And it brings the wild man out in me. I enter her from the back side and she arches her back for me shaking her sweet firm round ass, Do that again... oh yeah... oh oh oh yeah... we both yell out at the same time and stars explodes into our minds as we lay there while our bodies rocket out of control. And I swear I could feel every little sensation she was feeling the entire time and I got the impression she could feel mine. It was mind blowing hot steamy sex. This woman blows my mind. I've never felt anything like this before with any other woman. And we didn't even share blood. I want to see her again.

She turns looking at me sadly. She kisses me softly. I try to make it a stronger kiss already feeling myself growing inside of her again, wanting her again, already. She pulls away. "I'll get a hold of you as soon as I talk to my friend. I'll find you I promise.

"Shh but that can wait, for now I want you..."

"Times up!" she says sadly before I can finish my sentence.

"Time, what time?" I try to say, but before I can finish I'm landing in front of the Shitkick bar. I almost stumble into a drunk as he is walking out. Shit, I look down thinking I must still be naked and am relieved to see she clothed me first. I'm a little saddened that she used me and then threw me out so quickly without even a goodbye or see you later. We still had a while before dawn.

As I catch my breath then walk into the bar I see Marcus sitting there speaking with Buck. The thought dawns on me it had been exactly that – one hour.

"It's about damn time," Marcus growls handing me a shot of home-brew as I reach him succeeding in taking my thoughts away from Mariah for the moment anyway.

I nod. "Thanks," I growl back irritated then take the shot. I wait for it do its job and settle me down.

"What did you learn?" Marcus asks glaring at me, yet I can tell he's also relieved that I'm back standing before him instead of in the realm of the Gods.

I give my elder brother the run down in as few words as I can before leaving. I'm tired from the long day wanting to be alone for a while to get my thoughts in order, and my body back in control.

16

Forgiving

Issy

I sense him the moment he crosses his property line and I breathe a sigh of relief. Thank the heavens he's safe. I was beginning to worry not understanding why he hadn't returned with the rest of us, the five can appear anywhere with no sign of their coming.

Relationships…this must be why I've never been in one before. Much too complicated. Putting yourself out there to be crushed is for the birds. But oh what a magnificent feeling it is when it's going good, when he is loving you, when he's teasing you, ooh when he's pleasing you.

I take the brush from the vanity and begin to count as I brush through my long curls.

One - feeling spoiled that I'm in such a lovely house instead of my poor old Vw bug.

Two - the Vw wagon that is now lost from me forever,

Three - I feel a sting of pain at the thought,

Four - since it had been my home my shelter since the early seventy's,

Five - and my only way of escape for such a long time now,

Six - what will I do,

Seven - now when it's time to run -

Eight - I can't stay with Marcus, another sting of pain jabs me in the gut,

Nine - at the thought of leaving,

Ten - and never seeing Marcus again,

Eleven - Humbled, my mind turns back to him, blue star like eyes looking in to mine,

Twelve - I would never use these uncontrollable powers,

Thirteen - on purpose for myself,

Fourteen - but I would for him,

Fifteen - I have never been able to control these powers,

Sixteen - no matter how hard I've tried,

Seventeen - though. They just seem to show their faces,

Eighteen - and save me from whatever doom,

Nineteen - I'm in at that moment in time, twenty, and then just as quickly as they arrived they disappear as though they've never been there in the first place.

I set the brush back down on the dresser and peel off my clothes, then slip on the pretty, green silk nightie he bought for me yesterday while I had been waiting for my prescription. I had seen it in the window and had thought how beautiful it was, but never in my wildest imagination did I see myself wearing something as pretty as it. You don't dress in fancy sleep wear when your bed is your car. It was a little... well... a lot presumptuous of him to buy it thinking he would ever see me in it. But it seems it was meant to be... written in some book somewhere in the heavens, or where ever those things are written down and or assigned for us to come together. It was just a matter of time and we both had known it. The way we attacked each other was like a couple of explosive devices colliding. Nothing could have stopped us.

I hear Carra and Brenn's voices down the hall and my mind returns to earlier today. I didn't summons the power to lift them. One minute they were on the ground the next they were in the air, motionless. It happened because I felt threatened. It's the way it always occurs. And like always I couldn't control it. And that's what scares the hell out of me. It's impossible to make - what I call, 'the bitch from hell' inside of me - understand that I'm safe, before she lashes out to protect me.

I guess I'm just lucky I didn't slam them up against the wall knocking them out, or giving them brain damage, or even worse yet killed them the way aunt Callie had killed Zookie all those years ago. Damn it. What an embarrassing way to meet Marcus family. I'm surprised either of the women has forgiven me at all besides trust me. If it was reversed, I don't think I would be so forgiving. They realize I'm different and I can tell they think I'm a witch. But I'm not. I hope.

I hear their voices stop outside my door. Knock knock. I walk over and open it curious of what they want. "Hi. What's up?" I ask noticing their arms are behind their backs. Uh oh, what are they up to? They both look guilty as hell.

"We have a surprise for you. Come sit down." Carra say's pulling me towards the little couch. They sit on each side of me and I don't like being caged in like this.

Carra pulls out a bottle of wine from behind her giggling, while Brenn has Lindor chocolate. I smile.

"We thought you might need a little girl time..." says Brenn.

"So we brought our favorite girl time treats." finishes Carra.

"Why, what's going on to make you think that?" I ask, not used to being a part of girlie stuff like this.

"Don't be suspicious..." says Brenn.

"Yeah, we had a bad introduction so we want to start over and be friends," finishes Carra. Jeez they should be married the way they finish each other's sentences. I smile.

"We realize how badly we acted and will understand if you're not ready to forgive us," says Brenn.

"However we're both hoping you will," says Carra.

I giggle. "Do you two always do this?"

"Pretty much." They say simultaneously. Then we all giggle.

"There's nothing to forgive. If anything I've been concerned about you two coming to terms with me and what I accidently did to you."

"Here," Carra lifts the bottle of wine into the air, "let's make a toast to pretending our first meeting never happened."

"Cheers to that." we all say simultaneously passing the bottle around and taking sips. Then we share the chocolate and for the first time in my adult life I had real girl time, and loved it.

The girls told me all about Crucia's curse that Marcus had mentioned, then never got around to explaining. I'm shocked. "Here I thought I had it bad. I think you and Maximus had it much worse, Carra."

"Not just us, but our entire clan." She says, flashing her eyes to Brenn who is shaking her head in agreement.

"I can't imagine the same scenario happening for four hundred years, and all because of a curse, your supposed best friend, put on you out of jealousy. Kind of a love triangle scenario, you all loved each other in different ways, so it seems. Love hate so close."

"It was awful and the rest of the family didn't have it much better because their lives had been put on hold. Hunting Crucia, while searching for Carra, and once they found her she would always be plagued with amnesia. Imagine Maximus, trying to convince Carra, to fall in love with him time and time again."

"No offence Carra, but It must have been exhausting for him. The man is patient and loves you completely."

"Yes, it took its toll." She waves her hand ready to change the subject, "Enough about our family, tell us about yours, Issy." says Carra.

"Oh me, there's not much to tell."

"Oh come on... there must be something..." pipes Brenn.

"My family is all dead, as far as I am aware." I blurt out before I can stop the words.

"What...all of them?" asks Brenn putting her hand up to cover her heart.

"I'm afraid so, but if I'm wrong and any are still living they wouldn't know where to find me, and I don't dare try to find any of them."

"How can you be sure then?" asks Carra.

"I can't be sure. And it's probably better that way. I've never gone back home."

"Why do you think it's better not to find out if there are any still living?" asks Brenn, opening another dark Lindor chocolate.

"Because if I found out some were still alive I would be tempted to find them. If I tried the hunters would follow me, and I would never consciously lead them back to my loved ones."

"Oh, I see." They say simultaneously with dawning in their eyes.

I look at these two women so sweet and nice even though I found out the hard way they have a whole tougher, assertive, she devil side. They found out first-hand the same about me. I decide they would make wonderful friends and hope it can last a while longer because they are my first friends if that's what they really want to be.

I'm getting used to this family and guilt and regret are dancing around in my brain for bringing this kind of trouble to their friendly little vacationing town's back door. Most of them don't normally live here. However Marcus has this beautiful cabin and he stated he's on an extended vacation. I'm not sure what that means. Perhaps he doesn't plan on going back? And Buck and Sophia live here, all though, I guess there not really blood family. Either way I wouldn't wish this on anyone of them or the town's residence. It sucks this is my fault. The hunters followed me here and now I've involved all these nice innocent people. Whatever am I going to do? I must stop them, or lead them away.

"Uh oh looks like the funs all over girls, Marcus comes, so we should take our leave from his room." says Carra.

"Yeah I suppose I should tend to Treys feet a little more before we go to ground for the night. He needs extra healing and I want to be with him, yet he only agreed to go for the night. He's afraid to stay down to long, for fear of not getting his revenge on the hunters," agrees Brenn yawning as they walk to the door.

"Thanks for the girl time ladies." I say, as they open the door walking out.

"No problem good night." says Carra.

"We'll do it again." says Brenn. And just like that they're both gone.

I sense him behind me as he enters sifting through the window. He is tired and weary like me, I can tell. His breath is warm on the back of my neck and I crumble into tears as he slides his arms around my waist pulling me closer to him. Pride - shmide who needs it. Not when he's this close, and he smells so damn good, and I hear that deep sexy voice rumble in my ear.

"Shh," he comforts me resting his chin over my shoulder, rocking us. "It's ok now, I'm here baby."

"Baby!" I stiffen. "You think I'm a baby? You stay out all night after making love to me today. Which I'm not ashamed to say was my first time, as in ever. I was so worried about you, but hadn't even realized how much until just now!"

"You were worried about me Issy?"

I blush realizing what all I had just admitted to him.

He has the audacity to chuckle. "I don't think you're a baby, baby, but I like to rock and cuddle you. I like the softness of your skin as smooth and silky as a new born baby's." He rubs his hands up and down my back massaging it, 'oh yeah, he had me at Shh, just don't touch the spot below my ears or I'm done for, and there's nothing I can do about it.' He murmurs, "I need you." and directly afterwards kisses me in the exact spot mentioned earlier. My legs go limp.

I gasp, flustered trying my best to stay on track with this conversation. It's difficult to think straight when he's this close. I need air. I try to pull away from his ...oh so tempting arms and away from his hard persuasive body, but it's useless. How does he turn my brain to silly putty?

He chuckles. "I missed you too, Issy." then licks me there again.

I turn in his arms and close the distance between our lips reaching my hands up into his hair. Dark long hair loosening it from his tie at the back of his nape I want to feel it as it surrounds my naked body. I am lost. Umm his lips flavored like homebrew and I've decided the future's unknown, so I want to be happy now in this moment. "I could die tomorrow."

"I won't let that happen." his tongue glides down my shoulder blade.

"Or worst yet you..."

"Not a chance." his lips glide to my right breast.

"You can't be sure. It could even happen tonight." His right hand moves down my side over my hip and grabs a handful of my bottom drawing me closer to him.

"Nope ..." he nibbles at my breast and I start to float, "our schedules too busy for interruptions tonight."

"Oh is it now?"

"Yes, baby, perhaps even for a couple of days."

"Is that so?" I arch into him as my mind starts to slip away.

"Uh huh, raise your arms." He says tugging my blouse over my head. "We need to get you out of these clothes and into my bed."

"We do?"

"Oh yes."

"I want to bond with you Marcus, I want your blood." I burst out so lost in the moment. His hands and lips all over me I can't think straight.

He stills.

I hold my breath.

"Marcus."

He groans. Something between us has changed and is getting stronger. "Are you sure, Issy?" he gently takes my face in his hands peering into my eyes as if searching for the truth.

I nod my head.

"This can't be taken lightly. If we do this...if we share blood, it's forever. Are you sure you're ready to be my wife, my Eternalmate? We've only met yesterday." He adds quietly, softly.

"Answer me this. Would you have me be with another?"

He growls dark and menacing.

I nod. "You became my Eternalmate the minute I gave myself to you. Don't you understand Marcus; I have waited my entire life for you to come my way." I say as tears stream down my over emotional face, feeling happier than I've ever felt before. I'm going to be married. He lets go of me and I lose my head for a few moments doing a happy dance, turning in circles swinging my hips back and forth like a hula dancer. I get my wish after all, dreams do come true. Just like the princesses on Disney Channel, Cinderella, Snow White, Arial, Belle, Jasmine, Pocahontas,

Fa Mulan, Tiana, Rapunzel, Merida and Aurora. I will always have my Prince and we'll always have each other to hold on to and take care of for as long as we both may live, which is an eternity for us.

I stop twirling becoming aware that Marcus is awfully quiet and isn't joining in on the happy dance with me. I gaze back up into his starry blue eyes and am startled, my eyes widen, and I only see disbelief mixed with what I can only explain as confusion in his disturbed demur. And his shoulders are slumped as in defeat... But too late I spot the change in his eyes and comprehend the meaning in the words he had just spoken. He wasn't only questioning me, he is unsure of his own feelings and he was telling me he isn't ready. Oh God, I'm such a fool. Nausea overwhelms me; please don't let me barf, not now, not in front of him. He doesn't want me as an Eternalmate; he only wants me for sex.

As soon as I comprehend that news I quickly turn my back to him not wanting him to see the horror that I am struck with. I stand there for a brief moment unable to breathe my body trembling. Marcus tries to take hold of my arms denying what he realizes I'm thinking, as the truth.

"No, you've got it all wrong - let me explain. I want you more than I've ever wanted any woman and it's not only for sex. Which I might add you wanted that just as badly as I did. I do still. And if I remember correctly you didn't indulge the information with me that you were a virgin, of all things before the deed was done. I think that was a pretty important thing for you to share after waiting a hundred freaking years, don't you? But we have to figure some things out fir..."

I vanish before he can say another word. Sickened, I land on the other side of the lake and I fall to the ground and let myself vomit so sickened about the events. Then the tears begin. Like a faucet turned on high they pour from my eyes and I can't turn it off to save my life. How did I judge that whole situation so wrong? What was I thinking to push marriage on the man? For God's sake what made me think he wanted that? Did he ever give me any indication that he wanted me as his woman? As his wife, his Eternalmate to live with him for the rest of eternity! I've ruined everything; he now thinks I'm a freak show trying to push marriage on him.

I pull myself up from the ground where I had just puked and slowly walk the few steps to the lake in a daze. I get down on my hands and knees dropping my hand into the warm water cupping it to bring some to my face. First washing my mouth and then my entire head and it feels so much better. Next I bring some to my lips and gulp it down. It tastes awful but better than the barf.

What the hell is wrong with me? I think, confused. Hurt.

Just because he had appeared in my room...well, I mean his room? He thought we were just two legal adults enjoying mutual sex having a good time together. He had not even tried to share blood with me. He never planned for it to be for life.

On the other hand how does a woman over a hundred years old explain to the man she is about to have sex with that she's waited all her life for him to show. Talk about a deal breaker. He would have never made love with me and I would have never known what it was like to feel so special with a man I already cared for. Love at first sight. I believe it's true for I have never responded to a man the way I did with him. I can barely breathe when the man comes near me besides think. That's neither natural nor normal, at least not for me. Tears fall down my eyes again crippling me over.

My stomach lurches for the second time and I lean over losing my... what should have already been empty from the last time - gut, so sickened by my own insecurities, my own weaknesses, and my own naivety to think I meant more to him. I wanted his love so much I didn't listen to my instincts'. I was just an easy piece of ass and he was only helping me because this could affect all of us, not only me. Rightfully so, but still it hurts.

I'm such a fool. I might as well go to the hunters now and give myself to them as I had thought of before. Because I have nothing else to live for, nothing left to hope for, nothing left at all. Not even my trusty VW. I'll give myself today to mourn the loss of him and what could have been, but tomorrow I let the witch hunters find me. And give myself up to them. And this will finally end just like it should have when I was a child, and everyone else will be safe from them at last.

17

Angel of Suicide

James

"**J**ames! James wake up! James, you must wake up before it's too late. I need to speak to you. James, it's a matter of life or death. James I'm a friend of Mariah, I have an urgent message from her! Wake up now or you're not going to like what's about to happen! Okay, don't say I didn't warn you. BAM!"

"Oooooow! Son of a....! What the hell?" I wake up grabbing my head in excruciating pain as if someone just let a time bomb off from the inside. I fall out of my bed and on to my knees the pain is so unbearable I don't think I can stand and fight if I had to. I peer around me trying to get in a fighting stance. As the pain lightens I turn searching the room for something anything that could have caused my head to hurt like this. Then just as quickly as the pain arrived, it subsides. I sit on the bed relieved for the nuisance to be gone wondering if I have an aneurism, or something like that as I rub my noggin. I've read about them in one of those medical journals I like to read. My eyes flash to the mirror performing a quick inspection. I can rule out being hit by an object, no evidence to that effect. Hmm perhaps I should see a doctor later today. It could be from all the pain I sometimes endure from the premonitions.

I lift the blind peaking outside. It's still early so I decide to close my eyes for just a while longer to meditate.

Instantly I see a man that appears to be an angel with bright red curly hair, big blue eyes and covered everywhere in gold dust just as Mariah had been. There's one other difference though – this angel man has fairy wings. What the hell?

"James, Mariah requests your presence. She states she has life threatening information to tell you."

"Who are you?" I demand, opening my eyes and jumping out of bed.

"I am Jinx, the angel of dreams. Will you come with me?" he asks, appearing in front of me in a gold body suit just like Mariah had been wearing the other day. Causing me to wonder if they all have to wear the same get up. He reaches for my hand. I on the other hand move the other way growling.

"I don't think so mister, come with you? Come with you where? Are you crazy coming into my room and waking me up? Are you in a hurry to die?" My mind can't comprehend what this angel of dreams is doing here. And most of all why he's waking me up, hello dream angel – not awake angel. More importantly why does he think I would go anywhere with him? I take a step back not sure what this angel of dreams is capable of, wanting to grab those wings tie them in a knot and throw him out my window. Speaking of wings why does he have wings? Mariah doesn't have wings. And seeing him in the bodysuit of gold is nothing like seeing Mariah in one. It just seems wrong somehow.

"Mariah indicated it is imperative you come now, it won't wait until she can come to you at midnight tonight. She decreed it's urgent. She said it will be too late if you wait. Time is of the essence we must go now, that is if you're willing to save your friend?"

"Save who? What friend?" I demand my mind trying to grasp this weird situation. Wondering if I'm still dreaming and this isn't happening at all. It wouldn't be the first time after all me being a seer. "Is it Mariah, is she in trouble?" I ask wide awake now ready to go anywhere it takes to help her.

"No, it's not Mariah, although she does risk her own life, or at least her status by helping you. For that matter so do I," he says, scowling at me with his nose in the air as though he's wondering if I'm worth the trouble, "but Mariah is a good friend and if she finds this situation worth risking her neck over, so do I. Now for the last time will you come or not?" he inquires through gritted teeth as he reaches his hand out once more. I look at it skeptically.

"Do you really expect me to hold your hand, Jinx?"

"Oh brother, are you kidding me right now? Don't flatter yourself, vamp." Jinx says rolling his eyes, before laughing an all out loud echoing off the walls kind of laugh, so flamboyant in fact I'm surprised it doesn't wake the whole Skagit County, not to mention the people in this house. Jinx grabs my shirt sleeve so quickly I didn't have time to stop him, and we are whisked from my guest room at Marcus house, and appearing in the golden realm within minutes. Quick little shit! He drops me and I barely have time to land on my feet in Mariah's room.

"Good luck with this one," I hear Jinx say over head, "give me a jingle when you're ready for me to return him home. Make it quick though, my break is only a half hour. I'm just going for a Starbucks coffee. Do either of you want anything?"

"You have a Starbucks up here?" I say surprised.

Mariah giggles.

"Sure, I'll take my usual and get Marcus a special one," Mariah say's winking up at him as he disappears, and for some reason that wink pisses me off. I wonder how good of a friend this Jinx is to her anyhow, he must care an awful lot to risk his job and maybe his life for her.

"He's my brother." She answers my question as though I had asked it out loud, while shrugging her shoulders.

I glare at her, "Then why did he tell me he was your friend?"

She shrugs her shoulders again, "He's overly protective, and most likely trying to size you up. Are you happy to see me or not?" She asks opening her arms for a hug.

"Yes of course," I say as I take her into my arms, "but I can't help wonder why I'm here? Did you want a replay of last night so soon?" I purr, gazing into her wide, concerned, blue eyes. "By the way can all angels read minds, because I sense you and Jinx can read mine?

"Yes, pretty much." She winks, smiles, and then blushes.

"Well, that explains a hell of a lot."

"James I wish that was the reason that I sent for you. It would be much simpler, however I have bad news, and I figured you wouldn't believe it coming from a stranger."

"So it's true, someone's life is at stake?"

"Yes, you must act hastily."

"Tell me who it is. I can't help until I understand what the problem is." I say, drawing her in closer placing my forehead against hers and my fingers in her hair holding her to me.

"It's Issy. She's planning on committing suicide." She says in a whisper. "She feels hopeless."

"What, Issy? You've met Issy...how?"

"I made it my business to find out about your clan," her cheeks redden, "and if you remember right you told me a little about them last night. Besides, Issy is why the witch hunters are here. Until the spell is broken they will always follow her." She says matter-of-factly.

"I'd like you to explain where you got you're information about the hunters, and Issy's part in it in a minute, but first you've got that wrong concerning Issy. She's home with Marcus, safe right now. We came home at the same time tonight. He sifted through the window where she is staying. Hell, they're in love why would she want to do herself in when she's just found new love?"

"Yes, I have heard that to be true. None the less I asked my trusted angel friends to keep an eye on you and your family." She stops and gives me a quick sad smile and I am touched she cares enough to have her angel friends for all intents and purposes spy on us, yet alarmed at the same time that she is aware of Issy and her part in this mix. Marcus will be livid when he finds out!

Her spine stiffens and her eyes crease. "Hey, I wouldn't call it spying. I can't help it if I can read your mind. It's a curse if you ask me, and I don't like it any more than you do. "

"I was only testing your abilities, I wanted a reaction and boy did I get one. I had to see how well you could read my mind."

"Don't doubt me again. Now do you want this information or not?" she asks lips turned up all pouty. Probably because her little mind playing game is out in the open now. I will need to do a better job at covering my thoughts around her.

I nod.

"The angel of suicide is who came to me tonight. She stated that Marcus and Issy fought and she disappeared using her witchcraft, leaving no scent for him to follow. Her plan is to give herself up to the witch hunters. She trusts with her sacrifice the hunters will disappear and all will be well. As if they had murdered her at the same time as her parents. She believes herself to be the problem. She thinks if she dies Marcus and all of you will be safe from the hunters."

"Where is she now?" I ask, humbled strumming my fingers through her soft locks.

"The other side of the lake from where Marcus house is located was her last location. From what I'm told there is a small hidden shack in the trees. She is certain no one would look for her so close to his house. Issy plans on staying put so the hunters will find her. They always do, this time she doesn't plan on escaping." She puts her arms around my neck, "I'm sorry for such bad tidings, James. My brother comes, go, go find her, save her because if she dies," her eyes flash down, "so does your brother. He loves her it's his Eternalmate."

I nod as her lips come to mine.

All of a sudden that little shit Jinx has a hold of my shirt, and were flying through the air again not even enough time to tell her goodbye. Damn him! Although I think I heard her voice echoing, "I'll see you at midnight." He drops me on the floor of my room, hands me my drink that he got me from Starbucks, and laughs a wicked laugh. Then his face turns serious and eyes hard as liquid steel he says through gritted teeth, "You hurt her and I'll kill you. Just because I have wings don't doubt my power. Do you understand boy?"

"Boy...what the f...?"

"Yes, boy, I've been around since the beginning of time. And what are you a measly five centuries?" He asks with an arched brow eyes piercing, stance proud. Chin up.

All righty then, point taken, I think to myself wondering how powerful these angels are. "Yes," I say lifting my chin and squaring my shoulders understanding the way a brother thinks even though I don't have sisters of my own, Carrabella has always been like a sister to me.

"I don't plan on hurting her; we have an arrangement... that's all. That being said let me add I would kill anyone else if they tried to hurt her. We've only just met and I like her a lot. I have no idea where this is going, or even if it's possible to go anywhere at all, her being an angel and all. But that's something I'd rather discuss with her, if you don't mind."

He nods. "Then we understand each other. I hope you realize she doesn't typically do this type of thing."

"What type of thing are you referring too?"

"Pick up men. What did you do to charm her?" he says' with a piercing glare. "Did you hypnotize my sister?"

"No I didn't hypnotize her. And I wouldn't say she picked me up?"

"Then what would you say?"

"That is none of your damn business."

"She's my sister and has been through hell and back many times. I don't want her hurt again." he says getting in my space.

"What kind of hell?" I demand, standing up to him chin to chin not able to stand the thought of her going through hard times.

"Why should I tell you?" he asks, wide eyed with surprised look.

"Look... I care about her."

"You know nothing about my sister."

"Tell me." I growl, as he continues to glare at me and I become aware of the fact he's reading me even as I try to close my mind to him.

"Her life has been difficult and I wasn't always there to protect her. I am now. Don't doubt it."

Seeing red I grab him by the throat before I could think, "What happened to her, Jinx?"

"She was raped as a child, when she was still a mortal."

I growl letting him go and backing away barely able to breathe.

"It was by a much older man who was supposed to be her protector." He takes a deep breath, "The attack left her with child. She was just a youngster herself of thirteen. The baby was taken from her by the monsters family, as soon as she gave birth. She died shortly after of a broken heart. She loved the child no matter how it was conceived. She loves her still."

I stumble away from him. Raped? Child? My fists bunch at my sides and I have the urge to kill someone, the monster within showing his evil twin face. "Is he still alive?" I hear my self-ask wanting more than anything in this world to find the man and make him pay by ripping his throat out.

"Who?"

"The animal that raped her."

"No. I killed the bastard long ago."

"What about the child?"

"She's still alive."

"I saw no sign of a child at her house."

"She cannot live up there with us. Her attacker was vampire so her daughter still lives."

"No wonder you don't trust me."

"I wouldn't say that. I trusted you enough to give you some very private information. What will you do with it, I wonder?"

"I will help her if I can find a way. Where does her child live?"

"Salem." he answers, winking. Then he disappears before another word could be said. What the hell is it with him and the winking? I walk out of my spare room sickened by what he had said and appear at the door of Marcus bedroom, understanding the clock is ticking? I take a deep breath. What a day. Why am I always expected to be the barer of bad news? I'm hoping that Mariah, was wrong about Issy, and she's cuddled up to Marcus in his bed.

A second later I knock twice giving him warning as I walk in.

"What do you want?" he says, with a voice so broken that it causes me to nearly stumble as I walk towards him. Never have I heard his voice sound like this. Hopeless.

"She's across the lake in an old fisherman's cabin." I tell him getting straight to the point and then turn to leave.

"Where did you get your information?" the chair scrapes the floor as he stands up. Did you see it in your head? It was like the hunters. I could feel or sense no trace of her, or which way she had gone. She had vanished."

"No." I say shaking my head back and forth at the same time. "It's a long story one you don't have time to listen to right now. The short version is Mariah warned me. I'm tired and will explain the rest tomorrow. Go to her brother. I am told she is suicidal and plans to give herself up to the hunters when they find her. She won't try to escape them this time. She believes all of us will be safe then and the killing will all end with her sacrifice." He doesn't answer and I realize he is already gone to her across the lake. I smile. Wish them well and head for my room so I can sit and think some of these things out.

Phew. What a day. Issy suicidal, Mariah raped as a child, impregnated, and shortly after died of a broken heart when his family took her child from her. It's just too much for my brain to handle at one time. Plus, there's the other problem with Mariah. Marcus is going to have a shitfit when he finds out. It doesn't matter though. The angels can read our minds. There's nothing do be done about that. The facts are already out there for them to see. My problem is I don't understand what part they play in all of this? Why are they on the hunter's side instead of the people they hunt? I'll need to tell Marcus about these new facts later unless I can figure out a better plan.

I lay my head down on my soft feathered pillow and decide to take a short time to think, but my mind doesn't' give me a break. I'm in the grave yard walking towards the spot I met Mariah at last night. Somethings not right. I mean nothing looks the same.

I spot a woman wearing a cloak covering most of her body, hooded, yet I could still see some of her strawberry blond curls hanging over the sides. I recognize the woman, the red locks and the cloak. What is Issy doing here? She is supposed to be with Marcus. Did he not find her I wonder? I slip behind a tree to see what she's up to wondering if she plans her suicide for here?

She summons a woman, an apparition from the grave; she calls her Mother, Lily I believe is her name. They embrace and then the pair summons another woman, Meredith the demigod I heard them say. Lily and Issy slip chains around her the minute she comes out. They even bound her arms, hands and her legs. They don't trust her. Issy has the ability to use necromancy a form of magic involving communication with the dead either by summoning them or using them to foretell the future. Why didn't she tell us that bit of information, and why has she summonsed them? Another woman appears out of nowhere, another witch. Lily positioned herself in front of Issy's body, shielding her for some reason.

"Callie," I hear Issy scream excitement in her voice. "You're alive. But, but, how? I thought you were dead all of these years. Where have you been all this time?" I hear the happiness die down from her voice as confusion and then clarity enters.

"Stay back!" orders Lily. She holds her hand up prepared to use it like a wand if needed. They stand their facing each other. Lily with Issy tucked in neatly behind her, a mother protecting her cub. Lily's sister Callie looking ready to pounce, the problem is I'm not sure whose side she's on. And last but not least the demi-god Meredith. They stand in a wide circle glaring at each other. The two from the grave surprisingly still intact after so many years are mere apparitions and as far as I know they can't harm her, but the sister Callie can.

Out of nowhere the five hunters appear circling the women. Matthew, mark, Luke, John and Leviticus as Issy calls them, Ready to take the witches out, weapons held high. And I can't help but flinch. They're hideous and the smell. Holy crap is all I can think covering my nose.

There is a part of me telling my brain I must summons my brothers, for some reason I can't seem to get that done so enthralled with what's going on in front of me. I must save Issy is my only concern. I blink because the smell of these monsters' is so bad it's making my eyes water. Gross!

Skin hanging from their hundred year old bones. Can't they hide that shit?

I hear it long before I see them the sound of angels singing a sweet angelic old tune. They appear one by one in their little gold dusted jump-suits surrounding the group of witches, demi-god, and witch hunters. At least a hundred or more until I can't see what's happening anymore, they close in and make a tight circle. And I start to freak-out running towards the side of the group where Issy was at.

Mariah comes out of nowhere landing directly in front of me; her hands go to my chest. Whoa... with a lot more strength than was necessary, or I thought even possible from such a small creature. My eyes widen surprised to see her here even though I should have realized she would be here, we had a date after all. Nevertheless she didn't come for our date; this is about something much more meaningful to her. To all of them it would appear. I look up towards the crowd and see Jinx is here too. He nods.

I return the nod. "Mariah we need to talk later, but for now I need to help Issy." I say trying to move around her.

"James, this is out of your hands now," she says holding her ground, blue eyes serious with a hint of sadness. "This is between all of us," she adds boldly, points from herself to the all the rest of them in the circle, "to figure out. I thought when we first met you were here to help us, and to free the hunters from their hundred year torture. But you were not. You are here to kill the hunters saving Issy, and yourselves without even understanding the full story." She adds a look of determination filling her eyes. I need you to trust me and to stand down, James. We must finish this in our own way, by destroying them all if we have to for the sake of mankind." She adds sadly.

"What if there is another way with no blood shed," Issy asks walking towards us looking almost angelic, too. I silently wonder why the others let her through the circle, or if they even noticed her walking this way.

"We would be happy to listen, however I warn you if you try to kill the hunters we will have to kill you and all that try to defend you." Her eyes flash to mine, and back to Issy, "This ends tonight. Do you understand?"

Mariah asks her tone changed to a person in charge of the world around her. And I have to admit inappropriately as it seems, it really turns me on.

"Yes, I understand. I have summonsed my Mother, Lily, and the Demigod, Meredith, two women both of whom have put a curse on these witch hunters. My hope is that they will both revoke their curses on the hunters. Hoping then the hunters would have no need to hunt us and vanish. Therefore they would finally be able to go home to their families, to rest in peace for ever more, or if my guess is correct... go straight to hell - but who am I to say." she says in a voice unlike hers and I admire her way of thinking.

"Do you think they can be persuaded? Because from what I have seen of these two women even after having a hundred years to cool off, their hate is just as strong." Mariah states eyes clear as if she's trying to decide if it will work.

I hear loud talking in the other room and am awakened surprised to find I had been sleeping. I had been watching the future. And not been there at all. I jump out of bed and head to the next room. Never a dull moment is all I can think.

18

Reconnecting

Marcus

I fly across the lake like a crazy man and all I can think is, please, please don't let me be too late. Circling the area my eyes search for any sign. What will I say to her? What words will I use to get her to listen? I circle again once, twice, three times trying to get my scattered thoughts in order. And then determined I slowly glide down into the trees, drifting to the ground, shifting back into my human form. Landing directly in front of where the small shack is.

It's not the first time I've been here. I took note of it when I first moved here on a nightly flight when I was out getting some exercise. I've went inside to check it all out a time or two to make sure nothing evil was going on inside.

Taking a deep calming breath I walk to the door. I must act fast using the right words to keep her from doing the 'poof thing,' and disappearing without a trace again. What can I say to get through to her? Honesty is all I can come up with, I think, shrugging - if she will listen this time.

I walk up on the decrepit last remaining step of this old run down shack planning on knocking, instead at the last moment I appear through the door. I see her standing with her back towards me ear against the door. She sensed I was there. I take my chance before she has a second to stir realizing I'm behind her. I throw a binding spell on her, resulting in immobilizing her so she isn't able to vanish on me. I'm thankful Maximus taught me this skill a couple of years back, it has proven to be exceedingly handy.

I lift her over my shoulder as she tries to kick and head butt me whisking her away to my room. She tries again and I swat her very naughty butt lightly as she tries to kick me. "Stop it you little witch… this is for your own good!"

She is beside herself with anger struggling and fighting like an alley cat, but surprisingly she doesn't turn me into a frog. Of which I'm thankful. I'm pretty sure the only thing stopping her is because she can't as long as I have her bound by the spell. Because if looks could kill I'm sure she would have fried me by now.

I lay her on my bed gently not wanting to hurt her, understanding the ride across the lake with the binds was probably rather uncomfortable. The witch is angry though and tries to kick me in the face. Not very appreciative to a man who just saved her life if you ask me.

I shake my index finger at her, "naughty, naughty," I say with what I can only guess is a menacing grin because I'm very aware of how crazy I'm acting right now. I stomp over to my stool and pull it towards the bed. Then I walk over to my dresser pull out my hidden bottle of expensive brandy and pour myself a glass. I take a drink and just stand there my back to hers absorbing the rich aroma of the drink, trying to clear my muddled mind. What the hell do I do now? Shit, what was I thinking? Oh that's right, I wasn't thinking.

She has the audacity to growl; I turn my head towards her surprised to see she is shaking her head all about like a woman in an exorcism would probably do. I sit the brandy down on my small bar and walk back over to her sitting on the stool right in front of her, curious if she's trying to put a spell on me.

"Hmm," I say barely able to hold back the hysterical laughter bubbling inside me, "Issy, calm yourself - such a bad temper on such a pretty witch. I'm wondering if it would be beneficial or at least wise of me to marry you after all. I mean it will be tough enough having a half vampire for a wife, even though I am half vampire myself. But a witch will be challenging, don't you think? Oh...I'm sorry dear I've just realized you're unable to speak. Perhaps I should loosen those binds a little. Shall I dare?" she shakes her head in a yes. "Can you be trusted not to try and escape?" she nods her head up and down again, while I stare at her skeptically judging her body language and trying to read her mind. "I'm not so sure that would be a good idea... under the circumstances."

She growls again, brown eyes stormy with anger. And I get the feeling she's planning her vengeance as I speak!

Knock! knock! James is at the door. I get up from the stool and walk to the door thinking I owe him at least that after all he went through today because of us. I crack the door and squeeze through to the hall then shut the door behind me. I'm not sure if I want him aware of how out of control I am right now.

'I'm a little busy, what's up James." I whisper, while he says simultaneously, "did you find her?" I heard a commotion going on and wanted to make sure all was well." He says eyeing me suspiciously.

"Yes, she's here."

"Good, so she came willingly?"

"I didn't say that."

"What do you mean?"

I take a deep breath. Let it out. "The problem is I had to put a binding spell on her to get her here." I say frustrated, running my hand through my hair.

"Oh," James says eyes widening. "I can see where that could be a problem, especially if you plan to talk to her."

"Ya think?" I say with a slight chuckle, even though I'm frustrated. "Fuck, what am I going to do now?"

"Let her cool off for a while is my best guess." He says with a shrug. "That's what I would do anyway."

"Yeah, that was my best plan too." I say with low spirits. This is odd, because just a few minutes before when I was still in the room with Issy,

I felt happy in an odd sort of way. I guess, because I had found her and could keep her safe here with me. On the other hand our one way conversation we were having in there was going to get old real soon. "I want to talk to her, but I'm pretty certain at this point in time if I try to unbind those succulent sweet lips of hers, she would tell me to bend over and kiss her sweet little ass with them. Or worse yet turn me in to a ball of shit or something like that."

"Probably," he says with a tight chuckle. "I know what you could do while waiting for her to cool off." James adds eyes tired.

"Oh yeah, what's that?" I ask intrigued because right now anything sounds better than facing that witch in my room. At least until she has time to cool off and be Issy again.

"Let's go to my room, I'll share my bottle of homebrew with you and while I'm at it tell you a little dream I had just a few minutes ago." He has my full attention now.

"Why didn't you say so in the first damn place?" I growl.

"You needed to discuss other matters for a second, so I let you." He said crossing his arms in front of him. My first thought is he doesn't look real happy about the tidings he brings. That's probably why he wasn't in a big hurry to tell me about it. Ye gads, I hope it's nothing too bad, I don't think I can handle much more on my plate tonight.

"Okay, let me tell Issy, and I'll mean you there in a few minutes." A little bubble of hope starts to form in my belly. Maybe he has seen the answer or a way for all of this to end, I think walking back in to my room.

I walk to my dresser grab my bottle of brandy and my glass, not feeling the mood for homebrew tonight. Next I walk back over and sit in front of Issy. She still looks furious. "James had a premonition, so I'm going next door for a few moments. Don't worry you will be safe. Why don't you spend this time thinking things over and cooling off?" She glares at me as I get off the stool and start to walk towards the door. But for some damn reason peering into her sad, scared, angry whiskey colored eyes, I have a change of heart and want to get everything off my chest. I turn and walk back towards her sitting back on the stool.

"You went crazy on me, Issy. I couldn't hit rewind or fast forward. My mind was whirling when you were saying all those things. How could you not tell how I feel about you? I fell for you the minute I first saw you, as you leaned against the door singing out 'Hallelujah." I can't help but chuckle. "I know I must have told you that already."

"I'm not the type of man that does things quick, Issy. I tend to mull them over for a while, looking at all sides, options, and scenarios. You would already understand that if you knew me a little bit longer than just one day. In no way did I say I didn't love you, nor want you to be my Eternalmate... which is miles from the truth; I don't understand how you could even think it. Those are your own self-doubt. I was just trying to say I might need a little more time to figure things out. A courtship if you will. Old fashioned I realize, but then I'm a lot older than you, remember?"

She nods, her eyes misting a little.

"You didn't give me a chance to talk, besides spout my opinions. Or describe in anyway, how I was feeling. You just took for granted what you thought you read in my eyes. You might have been partially right, but I can gurandamntee you were mostly wrong.

Now do us both a favor and reflect about that for a while, and try to cool off while I'm gone. I'd like to take these damn binds off you, and talk to you like a grown woman instead of a disappearing witch when I return!" The truth is, and she doesn't need to be told, I am still a little hurt at her too, by her lack of trust in me and my character. I down my brandy pour another glass and walk out the door slamming it behind me without so much as even a glance behind me. My God I could have lost her tonight. The stabbing pain almost brings me to my knees as I grab my chest.

19

Men

Issy

What's going on over there? I strain my ear towards the door and all I can hear is the sound of deep muffled voices. The tone sounds important. I'm hopeful their not having a POW - wow making plan's to burn me on a stake. Even as I think it I am over joyed with the knowledge it isn't true. He said he loved me. Loves me - my heart warms at the thought and I swear I can feel the glow spreading through-out my entire body. And for some reason I don't understand -- I believe him. I smile to my self-feeling special for the first time since my parents died.

He came after me. I didn't think he would. I had left no trail for him to follow. And I'll be damned if he isn't right. It's not him, but my own insecurities that caused me to think that he didn't want me. Of course he does. I could feel it by the way he touched me so tenderly, and the way he talks to me so caringly, and the way he defended me against his own clan which is something not too many people would do. But mostly in the words he doesn't say at all.

I forgive him now that he's told me why he was acting like a crazy mad man. He thought he was losing me. He was scared to death when he couldn't find me. His only thought was to get me to safety. All he cares about is keeping me safe. I smile, letting that thought lighten the load of my mind. He wasn't trying to hurt me. Just breathe.

After all he told me my mind flashes back to the confused look on Marcus face last night. Now that I've had time to think about it I realize it wasn't an, 'I don't love you and therefore never want to see you again,' kind of look. Not a disgusted look that said 'I wouldn't marry you if you were the last woman on earth,' kind of look. It was more like a 'holy shit what just happened' look. I guess I can understand now why he had such a look on his face, it was really just confusion on how the conversation had turned so quickly from us having a semi-quarrel, to me thinking he wanted to become my Eternalmate. Psych! Jeez what got into me?

He is right. We just met the day before yesterday. I already had figured that out. This was my fault. All it took was one word coming out of his perfect deliciously shaped Elvis mouth, and in a heartbeat... my world changed. I was ready to be his for the rest of eternity. Wife – the word is so appealing if he is the husband. One thing is for certain, no matter how much I try, I will never live down that 'happy dance.' Talk about your embarrassing moments. I blush just thinking of how I must have looked to him when he wasn't feeling the same way. No wonder his face had been ashen. The man was scared to death probably going into cardiac arrest!

I wanted his blood last night. I crave his blood even now. And I haven't exchanged blood with any person since I was a child. Not since my parents were still alive. But Marcus's blood sizzles through my mind; the aroma that comes from him alone, makes me thirst for a sip. I need to share in every part that is Marcus. Why is the craving so incredibly strong? Perhaps because he is my first love, yet I'm not the type that there will ever be another. Then again possibly it's the fact he is my Eternalmate. Even if he hasn't figured it out completely.

I agree with him that we barely know each other, however with time we'll read each other's thoughts. I guess if we would have been acquainted longer than a day, it wouldn't have been such a surprise that Marcus was a thinker. He's one of those people who have to weigh and measure all his options a little longer than the rest of us do, before deciding on his path.

Hmm, I wonder if he is a Libra. Ugh, what's his birthday? Proof taken. But I love him and it doesn't take me days, months, or years to decide on things like that. After waiting a hundred years you just know...and I did the minute I saw him walking towards me at the Shitkick Bar. It was just after I had collapsed. The second time had nothing to do with the weather or lack of my Hemocil, and everything to do with the God I had seen before me...Marcus, and he caught me before I could land. The minute I looked into his starry crystal like blue eyes and smelled the sandalwood mixed with Irish spring of his body, and heard him whisper in my ear, 'I got you. Take deep, slow breaths and you'll be fine. You're safe with me,' I knew he was the one I had waited for all my life.

I barely make out the sound of the door opening in the next room and gather that the meeting must be over. Hopefully my original thought was wrong, and his clan isn't coming to get me, so they can prepare me for the stake and bond fire that waits outside. Oh please...there you go again crazy lady. He loves you...he said so himself. I beam remembering his spoken words.

He walks into the room slowly looking at me to gauge my mood, I presume. He wants to determine if I have cooled off. His shoulders seem a little slumped, which doesn't seem normal on him. He was seething and a bit cocky when he left. Whatever happened in the room next door has him down right defeated.

My heart beat quickens. What's wrong with him? What has happened? Oh God what has he learned that could have this effect on him? I don't like this face on Marcus, it doesn't suit well. I want to comfort him, so I try to inch closer. I can't because he has me in the binds still. Oh no...my eyes fill with tears. Shit! I don't want to cry in front of him. Oh no... Oh no...Stop! Too late they fall.

He stops in his tracks. He observes me for only a split second before I feel the binds lift from my sore body. He takes two huge steps, and is to the bed as I leap up and into his arms.

"What is wrong?

"I'm so sorry, baby." He says in a voice that cracks.

"Oh, please, no Marcus; I'm the one that's sorry."

"I thought I had lost you, forever," he whispers humbly using his thumb pads to wipe the tears from my eyes, so gently as if he was touching a baby's face. "I would have been lost without you. I can't go back to the life I had before now that I've met you. I was lonely and didn't even realize how much until I had met you, than thought I had lost you." He says searching my eyes like a child looking at his mother with so much love. He kisses my forehead and combs his fingers through my hair and away from my face.

I swallow hard before saying. "That reminds me, how did you find me, Marcus?"

"James."

"Oh, that's right; he is a seer, isn't he?"

"Yes, he's a seer. But he didn't foretell where you were. He can't control his abilities. The Prophecy's come and go at will. Most of the time it is of no use to him and he can't decipher what they mean, however sometimes he gets lucky and can warn people of coming events. He isn't able to ask the power to come, or command it to show him specific events of the future. But this was not a prophecy. His friends the angels told him where you were. And then he told me." He moves his hands around my shoulders pulling me closer to him while rubbing my back soothingly, my skin burns from his touch.

"Oh, I see. I think, James has angel friends? And if so, how did these angels know who I am, or where I was for that matter? I've never met any angels."

"Good question. I'm just learning about them myself, however from what James tells me they're lurking around everywhere, hidden waiting to protect mortals." His eyes change to concern and I swear I seen his eyes fill with water, before he quickly blinked it away.

"What is it, what's wrong? You're leaving something out." I ask concerned putting a hand on each side of his cheeks while looking straight into his beautiful stubborn blue eyes, so he couldn't turn away this time.

"Do you really want me to be truthful, Issy?"

I catch my breath. "Yes of course."

"Ok, you asked." He said with a sigh.

"The angel of suicide visited Mariah,"

I gasp, bringing my hands to my mouth as my brain starts shutting down, refusing those spoken words. Oh my God did the angel tell him what I thought about doing? My body trembles afraid of what he will say next. Brown eyes wide open staring into blue.

"Mariah, the receiving angel, is James new found friend. He met her at the graveyard yesterday, when he had hidden there to ask her questions about the Gods." He finishes looking at me sadly. "Baby, I was so frightened with what, James told me. I was worried I would be too late. That is why I flew across the lake and entered the shack like a mad man, binding and kidnapping you. Than worse yet spanking you as you tried to defend yourself. It sounds crazy, but I needed to keep you safe."

"Oh, oh, I a ...a...it was only a thought in weakness. I had already changed my mind." I cry meekly, ashamed. I can't believe he was told about that. How humiliating. He comprehends how weak I am now. I'm so ashamed. I try to turn away from his pity filled eyes. Oh God, he feels sorry for me. He gently takes a hold of my chin lifting so we're eye to eye. I look down.

"Issy, look at me."

I shake my head, tears slipping down my cheeks once again.

"Issy, don't ever hide your face from me. I can't bare it. Do not feel shameful. What you were trying to achieve is heroism. You were willing to give up your," his voice cracks again, "own life - for the rest of humanity. I am humbled by you. You are more woman than I ever dreamed of or deserve. Pure blood or not, I don't care anymore. I can't live without you Issy." He whispers and I am transformed even though I don't deserve his praise.

He doesn't hate me. He doesn't think I'm weak; instead he is under the impression that what I had planned to do was something to be proud of. I wish his words were true. My thoughts at the time of that decision had been muddled and scattered at best. I was upset and embarrassed. I think I had made that decision just to escape life. But how can I ever share that with him. The truth is I never would have followed through. Maybe, if I try I can do something to deserve his praise, though. I can't lose him that's all I care about.

Marcus clears his throat letting me know I've ignored him to long. I gaze up at him and grin, he smiles back at me and once again it alters my whole world on its axis.

"I'm going to claim you as mine, now." he says smoothly in his deep slow hum his sexy body riveting through my body.

"Claim me? What!" I say confused bringing my hands to his chest. "What do you mean...?" my eyes fly to his as the realization sets in, "Oh," my tongue darts out to wet my top lip; he wants to claim me as his own now. Star like blue eyes turning shades darker almost blue black meet mine. We peer at each other for a moment as our thoughts intertwine threading through each other's becoming one. I can feel our hearts as they start to beat in time in a slow blues like tune with every breath we take humming along in perfect harmony. But with every breath we take the beating gets a little quicker and louder thumping in our ears.

He licks his lips, "yes, you heard me right Issy; I'm going to claim you." He purrs pulling his shirt over his head, slowly, giving me the chance to admire his hard lean body. Oh my, I think, he's so damn hot that if he touches me, I'll melt right into his able hands. As it is a hot liquid steams through every vein in my body causing me to want him even more.

He stands looking at me as I admire every last inch of his wide shoulders, broad chest and roped abs and even further below to the thin strip of hair leading down, be still my heart. When I finally reach his eyes again I swallow, because they are smoldering hot. I begin to sweat from the heat bouncing off of him, into me, he grins.

"Your turn," he says voice low almost trance like.

"My turn?"

"Yes your turn. Take off your blouse, Issy."

I stare at him for a second consumed by him. The moment of truth is here. Is this what I really want, as in till death do we part? Eternity? I gaze at him a little longer and then his lips curl up and it hits me. What am I thinking? I don't need to think about this.

"Hell ya," I say standing up and grabbing the hem, starting to rip it off and over my head the same way he had just done. I want him more than anything I've ever wanted in my entire life.

"Ought...s-l-o-w-l-y, Issy." He grins eyes a deep swirling blue, darker than I've ever seen them. "I deserve a show too."

I pull it over my head nice and slow doing a little dance for him.

"Hell ya, is right," he says checking me out the same way I just finished checking him out. Slow and leisurely. He strolls to me then reaches his hands up to the clasp at the front of my bra. "Beautiful." He purrs next to my ear and my skin flutters from his warm breath. Eyes glowing as he lifts his big strong hands to both buds squeezing lightly.

He groans.

I moan.

He twists, pinching, and pulling. My head rolls back as his lips come to my shoulder kissing down my neck line and chest until he reaches my right breast. He suckles sweet at first than harder biting down, and It triggers something deep inside me making my inner thighs squeeze tight. I scream out and he stops for a brief second licking and suckling before moving to the right one lavishing it the same way. I hear my self-saying things I've never said before, bad things, naughty things, but I can't stop myself. It's all I can think right now in this glorious moment. I feel my self-climbing, my muscles tensing, reaching, wanting, can't quite get there. "Please, Marcus."

"Please, what... baby? Tell me what you want." He croons in my ear. Still lavishing love on my breasts with his tongue, his lips and his teeth.

I moan, "Please." As I reach for his manhood.

"Not yet." He slaps my hand away. Drats I want to lavish love on him too. It's my right.

He growls deep in his throat then let's go of me all together and I'm afraid he's changed his mind. My eyes fly open.

He stands back and worships me some more with that all too sexy look of his that says, I'm completely desired by this man. The one that makes me want to run and jump his bones taking him to the floor to do naughty things to him.

"Beautiful," he whispers in awe again. "Do you want me as strongly as I want you?"

I nod. "Oh yeah."

"Do you feel with all your heart as if the world will end if you don't have me?"

I nod. "You're not getting away this time."

"Do you think your heart will stop beating and you will die if we don't become one?" he asks his voice dropping octaves lower than I've ever heard it before.

I nod tears feeling my eyes.

He lowers himself to one knee taking both my hands in his; looking so hopeful it actually hurts me inside, in a good way. "Issy will you make me a new man and become my Eternalmate?" holy shit!

I jump up screaming, "Yes, Yes, Yes, more than anything in the world, yes!" I say as I reach my arms around his neck, tears sliding down my cheeks, happy beyond belief. I love this man so much. I start to do the happy dance. Than stop remembering what happened before. Shit. I turn to him eyes serious as my hands slide to my hips.

"Is this for real, I mean, no going back this time. We're getting married, sharing blood, becoming Eternalmates?"

"Oh no woman, like you said, there is no going back this time." He growls, eyes dancing, but oh so sexy. And then he surprises me by acting strangely doing something completely out of his character.

He slowly starts to move his hips back and forth as though he's enjoying the beat of his favorite song, and let me tell you the man is a sex God, Channing Tatum, Michael Jackson, John Travolta, Fred Astaire move aside because this man's moves have every muscle in my body singing. He starts to move a little faster turning and putting one hand in the air pointer finger towards the ceiling than the other goes up while the first hand aims pointer finger down, moving to the beat moving faster acting crazier and by the time he turns back to face me he purrs lips curled up, "aren't you going to join me in my 'happy dance?'"

I laugh my eyes glazing over as I join him in a happy dance. Then he slides his arms around me as we continue to slow dance around the room. Then his arms leave my waist traveling upward towards my breast slightly skimming over them and they tingle, yet he doesn't stop there, oh no he keeps moving up till he reaches my shoulders and lifts both sides of my bra straps, which I had forgotten was still hanging loosely from me, across my arms going backwards and clasping it in the back, where I can't move my arms.

"What are you doing?" I asked surprised.

"Shh," he says pulling me towards the stool, he was using earlier when he had the binding spell on me. Ha, now that I think about it he has me pretty much like that again. What is it with him and tying me up? He sits me on the stool carefully just at the edge directly in front of his long body sized mirror. He spreads my legs wide caressing them gently moving towards my V sending tingly pulses all over my body, he moves around me slowly rubbing my shoulders and back to where I can see myself spread eagle, breasts high with my arms tied to my sides snuggly. My inner thighs are burning my skin is tingling all over enticed to find out what he'll do next.

Oh my, what is he doing? I think to my self-body on high alert.

I try to look away uncomfortable seeing myself like this. Never seeing myself like this before. Wide open, spread eagle and it's a little scary. Suddenly the odd sensation of both ankles being tied to the sides of the stool reaches me, where I couldn't close them if I wanted too. I tense. This is scarier yet. What's he up to? I'm a little alarmed and even more aroused.

"Trust me?" he asks eyes deep pools of Smokey gray instead of his usual sparkling blue. "You know I would never do anything to hurt you, don't you?" I nod wide eyed. His lips turn up and he laughs that all out wonderful laugh, I had fallen in love with the minute I had first heard it, "you'll love it I swear. I'm going to do things to this sweet little body of yours that you've never imagined. And you're going to watch it all. "

I gasp.

"Kiss me, kiss me please. I can't wait another moment to have your lips on mine."

He walks back around to where he is standing in front of me, bends down and I'm so excited I close my eyes as his lips come towards mine. His lips touch them and then there gone. I wait a second for them to come back and when they don't I open my eyes.

He's there just grinning at me watching my lips frozen in time waiting for his to return.

I pout.

Then he winks at me, stands up, turns and walks away. What was that? That wasn't a kiss. That was a small appetizer only making me thirst for more. He walks to the bar and leisurely makes himself a drink, while I sit here facing the mirror spread eagle tied to the stool. Men. He takes a drink letting it settle watching me in the mirror, our eyes never leaving each other's. Would you like something to drink, Issy?" he asks as if this is just any other minute in any other day and I am not sitting spread eagle tied to a stool.

"No." I say feeling irritated.

"Sure you do," he pours me some blueberry desert blood wine. Returning to me he puts the wine to my lips and for reasons unknown I lean my head back for a sip, it feels warm and rich as it enters my mouth, and I keep it there just for a minute enjoying the rich taste, before swallowing it down. I feel coolness between my legs and I try to jump up thinking he's spilled the wine on me, forgetting that I was tied to the stool. I look down and see that he has placed a couple of ice cubes between my legs.

"What the..."

"Shh calm yourself. And be still damn it. He murmurs in his deep hum, and I start to feel chills run throughout the length of my entire body, and it's not in a cold way. It feels strange, but hot as hell.

He walks away again. Driving me crazy making me wait. I spot myself in the mirror, finally having the nerve to look up. My cheeks are flushed in a way I've never seen before. My nipples are peaked high and hard craving attention. I look wanting, another way I've never seen myself before. Music starts to play in the background, the blues. So that is what he was up to.

I glance down to where the ice is melting between my legs, a shiver runs through me and I feel Marcus watching me. I peek up into the mirror once again catching him watching me with lust in his eyes, embarrassed that Marcus saw me checking myself out, I quickly turn away.

"Look at me." He purrs. Don't be embarrassed because you looked at yourself. You're beautiful and you should never be ashamed of it. Just look at yourself he saunters up behind me voice low in that deep hum I love. He reaches his hands gracefully into my hair. Look at this beautiful silky, hair the color of a red sunset. I love to touch it twirling my fingers in it watching as it cascade down over your shoulders and breasts.

His hand moves to my neck "umm soft, sexy, perfect for biting, sucking, and licking," he smiles, "I especially love this vein right here." He runs his tongue across my main artery in my neck causing me to squirm feeling my blood heat. Then he moves on down my shoulders, "straight high and proud." He moves his hand to my breasts, squeezing them lightly, than pinching and twisting my nipples over and over again, as his lips peruse my neck and shoulders. I close my eyes as I begin to reach higher and higher wanting to be untied. Wanting to wrap my arms around his neck and spread my fingers through his hair. I moan. The ice melting between my legs cold hot, a sensation that's different for me. "Marcus I need to touch you, please untie me." I beg.

"Soon," is his only answer? "Look at yourself baby watch me touch you." He purrs in my ear. "Don't you like it, watching as I touch your body? Tell me the truth now baby, you like to watch, don't you?" One of his hands move from my breast slowly over the curve of my waist on down between my legs, cupping me his hand on my pelvis with his fingers covering my sex pushing lightly and pulling back and forth, and I scream out his name like a woman in heat, "Marcus!"

"That a girl, ride it out," my hips start to move up and down and the muscles there are pounding, wanting him to enter demanding his attention. "See there's no denying it, your eyes and body tell the truth. Say it. Tell me you like to watch me touch you."

"Yes, I stammer, yes I like to watch. Please Marcus please, untie me. You're driving me insane." I say almost in tears and I swear right at this moment I would give him anything he wanted, just for him to give me what I need. "Shh, not quite yet Issy." He says voice going deeper to the point that I realize this is affecting him too."

He stands and walks away from me again. Strutting like a wild panther to the bar. All I can think is he's doing this to me on purpose. Driving me crazy by making me wait. He returns with more ice wiping the melted ice away and setting more there. "Baby you're so hot," he whispers. Again I jump from the shock of the coldness against my - oh so tender needing to be fucked skin. Damn him. He pushes it closer spreading it all around my V and the coolness is more than I can stand. I lay my head back screaming his name once again as my body releases spasms shooting from me like magic and I can't control it. I just lay their rocking and rolling around as he continues to press the ice against me there. And he takes another piece to my breast rubbing and sucking and he orders open your eyes I want you to witness for yourself how I see you when you orgasm, how beautiful you look when you're so out of control, not holding anything back, so happy and I know it's all because of me.

He torchers me again and again until I think I can take no more and then I feel all the binds and the clasp of my bra in the back come undone. Freeing me he lifts me and kicks the stool out of the way. He stands me in front of the mirror having me put my hand on each side holding the frame. He makes me spread my legs wide and then he enters me fast and hard and I match him push for push, stroke for stroke, watching as he makes love to me caressing my body while he moves in and out both fast and slow, licking, sniffing, growling.

He has me move my hands down the mirror bending over still holding on to the frame as he moves his hand down and plays with my nub causing me to move my butt harder faster saying words out of control that I don't even understand, and then he pulls out gently turning me over as he enters me again face to face. I hear him call my name as I call his and we fall to the floor pushing harder reaching higher building climbing were almost there and we reach it at the same time. I feel his canines as they pierce my neck and mine automatically go to his upper breast. Our minds and our bodies are in another world now completely exploding out of our bodies, shooting everywhere like fireworks and I never want to stop, his blood is so good smooth and rich.

We place our left palms to each other's heart while the transfer takes place leaving us with the Eternalmate small heart imprint as we promise our love to each other forever more. I thought the last time was amazing, yet adding the sharing of blood makes it an out of body, no out of this world experience. We lay there folded into each other when were done neither of us wanting to move or let the other one go.

20

Destroying The Enemy

Marcus

I explain to Issy, all about James prophecy, and am not surprised by her raised brow and wide eyes.

"Me, necromancy?" she says placing her hands upon her chest.

I nod, "that's what he said."

"I don't believe it! He must be mistaken."

"Baby, I'm sorry but his premonitions always come true." I say, running my hands through her soft long curls.

"How does he decipher the difference between a dream and a premonition?"

"Good question. We've all asked him that same thing, and the answer is that the prophecies are more vivid and detailed unlike a dream."

"Oh, but surely he's been incorrect ...right?" she asks with hope glazing her eyes.

"No Issy, the fact is he's never been wrong."

"Never?"

"As in ever."

"So Treyvon was right after all."

"So it would seem."

We discuss the prophecy a little further before we decide on a strategy, too bad our first decision as Eternalmates is such a tough one. The problem is I don't like the plan. I down right hate it! The thought of Issy being a sitting duck for those monsters makes me see red! Its sucks James was woken up before he seen the ending of this scenario.

We arrive in Salem the next day after the groups involved had been consulted. Issy wears her cloak with the big hood that covers most of her body, her strawberry blond locks escaping the sides. She is stunning, so strong. so brave risking her life for everyone.

She walks around the grave yard until she finds the unmarked graves added years later than when they were murdered.

There's dates carved into the old tombstones, but no names, she tells me on our Eternalmate only line. However this is the area Mariah told me I would find my mom, it was so nice of her to help with this. And it is incredible the way her voice shimmies through my head. I love sharing this intimacy with her. She locates the graves closest to the time when their deaths had occurred. I watch her lay her head upon each plot with her arms spread open wide until finally she says, "I Found my mom."

How can you tell?

I can sense her.

She summons the apparition first of her Mother. Her mother is not surprised that Issy was capable of necromancy. They hug as best they could, her being an illusion and all.

"It's about time your realized you're a witch daughter mine. I am so sorry I was not able to tell you the truth before I was murdered. Callie and I had so many plans for teaching you how to control your powers. I apologize I wasn't here to help as you grew up."

"So I'm a witch?"

Lily's eyebrows shoot straight up confused for a moment before answering, "Of course you're a witch. How else could you use necromancy and bring me back from the grave?"

"I kind of wondered that myself. However, I was told by a reliable source, that I was not."

"Sorry about that. It was for your own good. A child can't give away secrets if she's never been told them."

"Oh that makes since." she says before explaining all that's occurred in as few words as possible. I witness the heartbreak in her mother's eyes even from where I'm hidden.

"Issy I doomed you to be hunted by these witch hunters your entire life? I... I ...thought I had saved you from them." Lily tried to embrace her daughter, but that wasn't able to happen. "Where was Callie? Why didn't she help you?" She adds with a furrowed brow.

"Mother none of this was your fault. You did everything within your power to save me. How were you to understand they had no idea of the difference between right from wrong? I never once blamed you."

"You're too sweet daughter, but thank you all the same."

Issy tell her the truth. I whisper on our private line.

I'm trying, but this is going to hurt her. She answers.

You must.

Ok, alright I'll do it now!

"Mother I'm sorry to be the barer of bad news, but as far as Callie is concerned, well, umm..."

"Well what. Spit it out."

"She's ...deceased. I never learned any of the details, but one thing's for sure she disappeared right after your death and she wasn't the type to abandon me."

Lily gasps.

"I'm so sorry mother."

"Callie dead! That's impossible; she's not in the afterlife. Your father is in the heavenly realm and so is the rest of our clan. And I'm a superior witch, and should always sense what's going on around me. Meredith chose to use them because their souls were tarnished. Forgive me." Her mom apologizes and the pain in her voice as it cracks is almost too much for even me to handle. Lily loves her daughter with all of her heart.

They continue talking for a few more moments and I tune them out realizing this conversation is too personal for me to be privy too.

"Mama I'm married now. And he's all and more of what I envisioned he would be. And everything you taught me that he should be. I waited for the perfect man like you told me to do. And like you said it would happen - it was love at first sight," That's when my ears perked back up and into what they were saying.

"Truly...? My baby girl all grown up with an Eternalmate. The last time I laid my eyes on you, you were still a little girl." she says eyes filling with tears.

"Yes. Mama, I'm a century now, can you believe it? More than old enough to be married don't you think?"

"No, actually it doesn't seem possible."

"Well I am, and you will love Marcus as much as I do." She chimes her face glowing. My heart swells so proud that she loves and trusts me to be the kind of man her mother always wanted her to find, as my eyes continue the process of scanning the area for any sign of the witch hunters to show.

Thank you baby. I whisper into her mind. Now you need to hurry things up a bit. From what James says the others should be appearing soon.

Her mother inhales, her spine stiffening. But this time it appears to be because she's overwhelmed with happiness. "Where'd he come from? Is he a witch? I'm so happy for you Issy, is he here? Will you introduce us?" she exclaims asking one question after another not giving my woman any time to answer her, as she searches in all directions.

Oh shit we didn't expect that to happen. When of course her mom would want to meet her daughters Eternalmate, especially considering this might be her only chance? Issy's mouth opens wide and her eyes haze over with bewilderment.

Say you didn't tell me you were coming here. You were afraid I would disapprove. I intervene into Issy's mind.

I no more than speak those words when I spy the clarity dawning on Lily's face before she speaks again, "well, obviously he's not here now." She say's pretending to search the grounds again. "Next time, OK."

"Yes mother he'd love to make your acquaintance when next we meet."

"Now, why did you bring me back from my grave? What do you need from me? I will do anything; anything that is possible for me to do." All I can think is good cover mom. She evidently realizes I need to stay hidden to protect her daughter.

Issy explains to Lily why she is here, and what she needs from her to help invoke the curse. The two of them work together to summons the other woman in this trio, Meredith, the nemesis who had started all this trouble in the first place. Lily and Issy ambush her the moment she ascends from the grave. They use invisible break proof chains to bind her hands and her feet. They don't trust her. Although it does no good because she is just an apparition and the binds are worthless. She couldn't hurt them if she wanted to.

It's hard to believe my Eternalmate carries the ability to use necromancy a form of magic involving communication with the dead, either by summoning them or using them to foretell the future. She didn't tell us because she didn't have any knowledge of it herself until James prophecy, the funny thing is her mother nor Meredith seems surprised by it. They recognized how strong her powers were to be even at the young age she had been at the time of their deaths.

Out of nowhere another woman appears. Aunt Callie, I presume, and the three women in the family could be triplets. Lily moved in front of Issy's body trying to do her motherly duty and shield her daughter.

"Callie," I witness Issy scream excitement in her voice. "You're alive. But ... how? I thought you were dead all of these years." The words stumble out of her mouth as though it wasn't already predicted to happen. "Where were you all this time?" The happiness dies down as she searches her aunt's face and I detect she is no longer acting. The reason is important to her.

Callie just stares at her blankly with an evil scowl.

"Stay back," orders Lily holding her hand up prepared to use it like a wand if needed although in reality there is nothing she could do at this point to protect Issy, from her sister. That is my privilege now. I think grimacing. I must keep her safe at all costs. The four women stand there facing one another. Lily with Issy tucked in neatly behind her, a mother protecting her cub just as James had predicted. Aunt Callie is ready to pounce the problem is I'm not sure whose side she's on, and last but not least the Demi-God Meredith all standing in a small circle glaring at each other.

If looks could kill you'd all be dead.

There's a lot of hatred here, tis true.

Be careful. I don't trust dear Aunt, Callie.

I don't either, and I can tell my mom is furious with her.

The two from the grave are mere apparitions and as far as I know they can't harm you, but Aunt Callie can. I'm edging closer to you as we speak. I say on our special line wondering what Callie has been up to all this time while Issy, so desperately needed her.

Then just as foretold the five hunters appear surrounding the women and my heart aches again at them being so close to my woman and her mother. Matthew, Mark, Luke, John and Leviticus, as Issy named them. They are armed and ready to kill. And I can't help, but flinch as I move closer through the trees and bushes. Their hideous just as I remembered from a couple of nights ago. And the smell oh my heavens the raunchy smell. Holy crap is all I can think covering my nose with my sleeve. How were they able to hide that from us before? I silently wonder if their aroma is what they use to kill their opponent's with.

I hear the angels singing their sweet lullaby just as James had foreseen long before I see them. They appear one by one in their skimpy little jumpsuits and all I can think is, 'good God, James wasn't kidding these outfits barely cover anything.' On the women it's fine, but a little distasteful on a man.

Hey, remember I'm in your head! Says Issy on out private line.

Woman, I've only got eyes for you. Now concentrate on what's happening around you, and shout at me if I need to come sooner than discussed.

The angels surround the group of witches, Demi-god, and witch hunters. There are at least a hundred or more closing in until I can't see what's happening. They squeeze in shoulder to shoulder fencing them in a tight circle. No one was leaving. And I understand what James meant now. They are so tightly threaded together that I can't make out anything besides them. It's a barricade and my heart speeds up, my stomach nauseated. It's hard not to freak out and it takes all the control I can muster not to jump over them all to reach her. There's no choice, I must trust these angels whether I like it or not.

Then my clan appears. I join them and together we fly over the gold dusted figures. I land directly behind the hunter who is standing closest to my Eternalmate. The rest of my family lands behind the other hunters, who surprisingly only focus on their masters. The hunter's beady eyes slide from Meredith to Lily as if they were robots. They don't seem to even be aware of our appearance.

"Stand down," commands Lily hands in the air.

Meredith is as confused as the hunters searching all around like she's thinking, 'what the hell is going on and how did I get here?' Her eyes settle on Lily and hatred sizzles in them.

Callie lifts her arms in response to Lily ready to battle and I sense something bad is about to happen.

"K-I-l-l T-H-E-M!" she bellows as I throw a shield around Issy and her mother not sure of whom she wants to kill who? Everyone peers at Callie in question. Lily appears to be furious and I swear I can see it coming out her ears because her powers are useless and it's obvious she's not used to being helpless.

"Issy you can end this here tonight. The power is in you begging to be released, use it." Lily shouts to her daughter.

Issy shakes her head back and forth. "No mother, I'm not that strong. Why do you think I disturbed you from your peace? I need your help."

"No, you don't. As I burned I transferred what was left of my powers to you. You are the superior now. You have been since my death. You can do this!"

"Mother I fear you have put too much faith in me."

"Don't tell me you can't feel the mightiness that lies within you waiting to be unleashed. Close your eyes and let it flow through you."

"Me the superior witch, I don't understand. Isn't Aunt Callie next in line?"

"No, my mother decided a long time ago that Callie should never be superior. She told me you were the next to rule as soon as you were of age. I agree with her. The ruler has to be kind and strong at the same time. She needs to be a true fair leader."

"What if I am none of those things?"

"Oh honey, my mother was never wrong. Now decide what it is that you want to happen and make it so. You are more powerful than any living creature on this earth. Use the element's earth, wind, fire, and water. Whatever you command will be done, but Issy this is the most important part - only use it to do goodwill towards others."

"Mother I can't control these powers." Issy cries out.

"Yes, you can. Be strong daughter. Be the woman I know you are. Marcus and his clan will protect you while you make it so. You are a smart woman. Use your brain, think, what is the best way to end this fight. How will all mankind benefit from this. You are capable daughter mine. The truth lies inside you and you can see it can't you? Do it now." Lily reaffirms.

Issy nods her head up and down. "I will try mother." Issy puffs out her chest hands rising slowly and mightily into the air her adrenaline growing and I feel the ground beneath me shake and this time it's for real. Everyone looks down jumping from foot to foot trying to get a strong hold. It feels like an earthquake the ground is rippling underneath us. Thunder - lightening, wind, rain whipping around us angrily - trees splitting from the force and splintering like a shower over our heads. And yes, fire begins to roar its ugly head. She's in a trance and I don't know if I can bring her out of it or if I should even try, yet I fear if I don't do something we might all die today.

Meanwhile while all this is going on I hear Callie demand, "What have you done? You passed our mothers powers to a child. Are you completely insane?"

"Oh no, Callie, I am dead. Remember? Speaking of which where were you when that occurred and furthermore where the hell have you been all these years: why weren't you here for Issy?" she spats as the lightening cracks its mighty whip and the thunder rolls the sky darkening by the moment to the deepest of blacks.

"I was hiding of course. Where do you think?" Callie answers.

"I think you ran and hid like a snake in the grass instead of helping my daughter." Lily spats.

"I'll tell you where she's been." pipes in Meredith smugly, finally finding her voice.

"Like I'd believe anything that comes out of your lying, filthy, mouth." Hisses Lily.

"That was always your problem wasn't it Lily. You always thought you were too good to listen to anyone. That's why I could never use my powers of persuasion on you, so believe me when I say your sister is not..." Meredith tries to say.

"Oh please, shut up you evil wench," sneers Callie.

"Now wait one damn minute, if I'm evil than so are..." Meredith tries again, but once again Callie interrupts her.

"Lily, you going to listen to this lying bitch, or me your own sister?" shouts Callie over the storm as it gets louder and more forceful.

"I don't know sister, why don't you let her finish a sentence. What are you so afraid of coming out of her mouth? What havoc did you cause this time?" fires Lily.

"Listen to yourself Lily, this Demigod," she pointed at Meredith, tricked your beloved, Jonathan and you over a hundred years ago, killing both of you, and you'd believe her over me?" bellows Callie angrily.

"I didn't say I would believe even a word of what she's said, but what bothers me the most at the moment is why my only sister won't tell me the truth of her whereabouts all this time. Where were you when I burned and while my daughter was all alone needing your help, and love? Why the hell weren't you there for your only niece? The one you swore you loved so much?" Lily demands with contempt.

"She was with Gabriel," taunted Meredith rudely interrupting.

Lily turned to Meredith in shock, "Who?"

"Gabriel..."

"The angel?"

"No... No, don't listen to her. She lies." Interrupts Callie once again, still trying to maintain her innocence, but her eyes show the lie she tries to hide.

"Uh oh, the cats finally out of the bag. Don't tell me Callie didn't tell her own sister about her big bad boyfriend." Spats Meredith.

"Shut up spirit. You know not what you're talking about." Screams Meredith over the storm, as she looks toward Lily.

"Oh did I forget to mention that Gabriel her lover was also one of the witch hunters?" Meredith spats proudly as I see Lily's eyes snap to Callie's in disbelief.

Lily gasps eyes huge and full of pain before it switched to fury.

"Please, don't believe her, it's not true. Trust me Lily." Callie says, but without much force behind the words.

"The leader in fact." adds Meredith.

"She's in love with him. Aren't you Callie? Speak the truth for once and quit blaming it all on Me." demands Meredith, cackling.

"If you weren't an apparition I'd kill you all over again, Meredith." Callie says with a hiss.

"Tis true than?" retorts Lily.

Meredith chants. "Somebodies in trouble..."

Callie looks into Lily's eyes with so much hatred that if she wasn't already dead, I fear it would have killed her all over again. "Life was always so easy for you wasn't it sister? Life was grand. The world worshipped you..." Callie tried to say, but Lily interrupted her.

"Worshipped me --- they burned me alive!"

"You were the Superior! All the covens worshipped the ground you walked on. Lily the good witch could do no wrong. You had Jonathan a man that every woman wanted eating out of your hand, but you did not protect him, did you?"

"So that's what this was about. You wanted Jonathan all along?"

"You let him and all the others die. What kind of woman lets her husband die besides a superior?"

"Let him die...?"

"Yes, let him die. You could have protected them all, but oh no you were too good for that weren't you? What was it you said? 'A good witch must never use magic to harm others.' Whatever sister, you let them die -- just as I let you burn!"

"You?"

"Tell me - how did it feel your skin burning from your bones?" Callie spats, with venom drooling down her lips.

"How could you? We are sisters." Asks Lily, sadly.

"Once we were sisters, but that bond ended long ago when you were not brave enough to save our parents."

"I was a child."

"You were the Superior! Nonetheless, now I will do what I should have done years before and kill your daughter taking what is rightfully mine. I should have always been the Superior, you were not worthy. You never had the guts for it."

"You would kill your own niece?"

"I will do whatever it takes for the right person to be in charge. And that's me." Callie states as though she's talking about something that doesn't matter at all and not Issy's life.

"You can try, but you will never succeed! Issy is much too powerful for you." growls Lily.

Meanwhile Meredith keeps cackling louder and louder just like a psycho bitch crazy lady trying to echo louder than the storm. She's ecstatic she has turned them against each other.

My overly sensitive ears are beyond hurting as I feel the blood trickle from them knowing my ear drums have burst from the horrific noise. The storm is so loud now I can barely interpret anything at all; the sounds are close to becoming one solid noise all rolled into one huge drum. I feel the fury as it takes the beast over bringing me to my knees.

In response to Issy and everything I've just heard said, I feel the anger rising inside me and the growl so fierce mighty and loud that everyone can hear it even over the horrific storm that's surrounding us in all directions. Louder than the thunder, the earth crumbling and trees splinting into pieces. I can't tell if it's the bear, or the wolf, or the man, but one thing for certain all three will kill anyone that threatens Issy, or her mother. And Aunt Callie might be the first to die.

Pain shoots through me as the beast's teeth erupt out of my gums rearranging my mouth so painful I almost pass out. Excruciating spasms rivet through my entire body as it is ruthlessly transformed from a man into what I'm not sure, but can only guess something in between a bear, a wolf, and a man. I must appear hideous something like Jekyll and Hyde and I can't bear to look at Issy.

"What's happening to you?" Maximus asks, a little short of breath as he tries to help me to stand.

"I'm not sure, but I think the beast is taking over."

"So I figured. We thought it might happen sometime and now it has. BTW - you look like shit. Are you safe to be around the woman folk?" He answers standing in front of me and Issy keeping us protected while we are unable to protect ourselves with Issy in a trance and me transferring into a beast.

This is horrible and not a way that I want my woman to see me. I can't stand the idea of her being afraid of me in anyway. She mustn't see me like this." I whisper on our bloodline trying to endure the pain still shooting through me.

Don't worry I'll make sure she doesn't, he says. Now hurry up I'm ready to kick some ugly hunter ass!"

My nails grow to the length of knife blades and I am now a killing machine stronger than the super hero, Wolverine, from the Marvel Comics. "Come and get me assholes!" I roar belligerently when I am able to stand on my own two feet again, and surprisingly that's all I have -- two feet -not four. Still a man I guess, maybe close to a grizzly and the battle is on.

A war of dance as all the players positioned themselves between the ones they chose to protect, but Issy and I stayed back to back her causing the storm from hell me causing hell here on earth. Swords in hand my clan swung them high and swung them low, but the hunters were quick for being so big.

Maximus was throwing fire balls, "Here catch this you nasty smelling pieces of shit." I catch Maximus yelling as he throws a fireball that missed them completely.

How can someone so big move so freaking fast? Treyvon asks on our bloodline breathing hard as he tries to stab a hunter who moves out of his way at the speed of light.

The angels are no help at all, says Anthony.

I'll second that motion, I say. They are dancing among us, appearing out of nowhere, directly in front of us, and then vanishing as fast as they came.

It is chaotic. I suppose they're still trying to keep the hunters alive. James adds.

If one more of them appear in my face, I swear I'll rip out their throat. This isn't a game. I say.

As soon as the next hunter turns my way swinging his mallet sized fist I duck then sink my knife like nails into his heart squeezing tight as the squishy like moisture, not blood its thick and black green instead of red. It's slimy and the odor is enough to bring even the beast to its knee. I surround my hands yanking it out holding my breath before he could make his next move.

Damn brother, that was sweet, says Maximus. Where do I get me a set of nails like that?

You can have mine as soon as this is over.

The hunter falls to both knees looking at me in horror. I hear a couple of the angels scream, "No," and as I let go of the hunter he falls to the ground dead. I turn to reach for the next when my peripheral vision spies something strange. I glance back to where the hunter was laying a moment ago and am surprised to see him standing again looking as fit as a fiddle. The spot where I had ripped out his heart is just as it had been before I had done it. "What the...? Impossible!" I whisper under my breath a little freaked out.

I duck out of his way as he comes towards me again. "I ripped his heart out, but he's still alive." I message my clan.

"What? Well how do we kill them then?" messages Anthony.

"Maybe if we should in-flick head wounds like they do the walkers on, 'Walking Dead?'" spouts Maximus.

"If the angels would stay out of our way maybe we could make that happen." Snarls Treyvon.

"I thought we weren't supposed to kill them, but help the angels capture them instead?" remarks James.

"Well that's easier said than done, when they are trying to kill us!" Maximus shouts.

"Issy said they can't be killed, so were slowing them down a bit, that's all.

Meanwhile as I dodge another hunter I glance at Issy, she stands proudly her cloak and hair flying wildly around her and I don't think there's ever been a more beautiful sight. Her hands still waving in the air as she chants words in some tongue she's probably never used before. Her concentration is mighty as if sculpted from kryptonite and I don't think anything could break it. I'm not leaving her sight until she is done. My only goal is to protect her at all cost.

We stand our ground no free pass for anyone even as I wait for Aunt Callie to make her move on Issy. Meredith is not a concern because she is only a ghost, but Callie's been waiting for a long time and we cannot let her succeed. Out of nowhere a bright light blinding us appears straight from the heavens. It shoots straight down the middle of all of us. I jump back while at the same time try to focus my eyes. The light causes chaos all around us. We're all blinded, no one could move, basically frozen in place.

A goddess appears slowly gliding down riding the light as if she were a surfer riding out a big wave. "It is time Meredith. Come home." She puts out her heavenly hands and we all glance from her to Meredith.

Than Surprisingly a God like giant appears behind her smiling serenely he put his arms around the goddess. A moment later Meredith arises from the ground no longer an apparition, but a goddess herself dressed in white silk. She rises slowly towards them as they both reach out their welcoming arms to her and I can't glance away to save my life.

I should be doing something to intervene, but what do you do when you're dealing with the Gods? The curse - the curse what about the curse on the witch hunters is all I can think, but the problem is we are all frozen and couldn't move if we tried. When she finally reaches them they embrace a family together again. Much to my astonishment 'poof' they all three disappear along with the light which blinds us all again.

Everyone staggers blindly for a moment while our vision clears. My eyes fly to the middle of the group frantically searching for Issy. There she is lying across a man's lap with her mom holding her hand and I cannot see her face to see if she's ok.

Wait a minute, rewind. Her mother is changed to her true form the same as Meredith was, but what surprises me the most is my old friend Jonathan is the man. What the hell? Where did he come from? Issy said he had met his demise many years ago.

I turn peering all around making a mental note of where everyone else is now located. My clan is all standing, the angels are everywhere, Issy's family is here, but where are the hunters and for that matter where the hell is Callie, the witch? But I don't have time to worry about that now, my brothers will handle them for me I think as I sprint towards Issy, as I see the tears on her parents face.

I appear before her taking a knee and place her hand in mine. Her eyes are closed and she doesn't appear to be breathing. "Issy!" I shriek my voice cracking. She doesn't move and I am horrified. Her mother is crying.

"No, no, no - please this can't be. Issy wake up." I sob crumbling to her side. "Wake up Issy, don't leave me. It cannot end like this baby, open your eyes and look at me. See me - I need you. Come back to me." I add taking her from Jonathan and laying her on the ground before going towards her lips for mouth to mouth as the beast finishes leaving my body. One two three I pump, than blow, pump than blow.

"YOU!" Lily screams. My lids open long enough to see her pointing behind me, while, Jonathan stands with the fury of hell to come burning in his eyes. "You did this! You killed our daughter!" adds Lily.

"She is not dead," I growl at the same time as Jonathan, between breaths hoping to hell that it's true. She is half witch too and I don't even want to think about the ramifications of that.

"We vampires don't kill so easily, do we, Callie? Not unless we're betrayed by someone we trust, completely. Isn't that right, Callie?" Jonathan asks in a deadly calm voice and I recognize the fact that she was the one who had helped Meredith betray them.

I don't need to peer up to discover my brothers captured Callie and Maximus placed a binding spell on her. "Issy, come on baby - you can do it. For God's sake open your eyes for me." I beg over and over rocking her body.

"Jonathan, believe me, I had nothing to do with your death. I promise you." I caught Callie say in the outer realms of my being my head spinning as though I'm in the middle of a cyclone moving farther and farther away from everyone, but thoughts of Issy. I will die if she is dead, because I can't live without her.

There's shouting all around me and someone's pulling at my arm, but I am too far gone to care. I scream to the Gods, "Take me in her place. She is good. Leave her on this earth so she can do good will. Take me!" I beg, "Take me instead!" I bellow and I cry until my throat is dry and bleeding and I can yell no more. "I will do anything." I add as I fall to the ground my head on Issy's chest planning on lying there until I die along with her.

The sky opens back up and the God of light says, "Be still. Go home; the hunters are no longer your concern. They've been released from the spell and placed to rest. Take what is left of your lives and live in peace. Meredith will not return to do you any harm. So it is -- so it will be -- this is my pledge." He blows a whistle and all the angels fly towards the sky in pairs.

"Mariah," James calls out.

"I will find a way back to you, James, one way or the other. I will return to you." Mariah calls back to him. As they all disappear and the sky begins to close behind them.

"Wait!" I yell panicked, sitting up and opening my eyes, "What about Iss..." her hand squeezes mine before I finish the sentence and I peer down at her. Her eyes are fluttering open. "Oh thank God!" I say as tears fall down my cheeks.

"Ddid it wwork?" Issy asks."

"Shh don't try to talk just now." I say wiping my tears from her sweet exhausted face.

"But..." she tries again.

"Shh..." I soothe.

"Please, did it work?"

"Yes Issy, it worked perfectly." Lily answered. "I told you, you were capable daughter mine. You had the power all along."

I searched their faces trying to decipher their conversation, "The storm?"

They both nod.

"The Gods?"

Another nod.

So you caused the storm to get the Gods attention?"

A grin, "Yep, I sure did."

"You disobeyed me?"

A nod.

"Well I'll be damned." I say, as I let out a laugh I'm sure echoed all the way into the realm of the Gods.

Moments later Maximus clears his throat behind me before saying, "There's still a small problem to deal with."

"Hmm?" I turn my head his way still delirious in my bliss that Issy is alive. "Oh yeah, dear sister Callie, what shall we do with you?"

"What do I care? He's gone, and this time he won't be returning," Callie said with hatred filled eyes and a foaming mouth.

"Burn her!" demands Lily and Jonathan simultaneously.

21

Happy Endings

Issy

*I*t's been six months since the terrible events that occurred at the grave yard, and life is better than I ever dreamed possible since that day, I think slipping on my favorite red tennis shoes. I need to go and find Marcus he's been spending many hours away and I miss him. He won't tell me what he's up to no matter how much I bicker at him. He replies 'man stuff' when I ask.

Marcus and I are having our official traditional mortal wedding tomorrow even though we are already married in the eyes of our kind, and I am blessed with the Eternalmate heart imprint on my left palm to prove it, I think looking at my left palm smiling because Marcus carries a matching one on his.

I'm so excited our families will be at the ceremony. It will be a small celebration Marcus's brothers and their women, his parents, my parents, Sophia and Buck. The wedding will be beautiful in a way I could never have dreamed possible.

My parents will be at my ceremony, I think again still having a hard time believing the words are true. That in its self is a miracle and I find myself saying those words over and over each day, so afraid that one day I'll wake up and they will be dead again. But I won't think that way now. No only positive thoughts allowed today.

My mom is so excited and can't stop planning, planning, planning. I think she's trying to make up for lost time and I love that about her. I don't mind if she wants to do all the planning because it's not my thing and if it makes her happy it makes me even happier for her.

A summer wedding how precious is that. Fresh cut flowers in mason jars, fruit picked early that morning in baskets and homemade wine made by Sophia and Buck. I was surprised to discover they made their own wine and it is absolutely delicious.

I spot my mom walk past the front window and the determination on her face reminds me of how rough the last few months have been on her, dealing with all the revelations of that dreadful day months ago. Dreadful yes, but at the same time my parents were given back to me. Terribly selfish of me, but I'm so happy their back in my life. So for me it was a wonderful day. A day like none other and it would take something earth shattering to ever change my thinking.

As a matter of fact for my mother it was the day she was given back her life not to mention my fathers. On the other hand it was also the day she discovered her only sister hated and betrayed her. Callie hurt her more than anyone else ever could have. And she made her burn for it. I still can't believe that it's true, but my parents were adamant about that. She could not be trusted and she had been a detrimental part of having many people murdered in the exact same way, including both of them and the rest of our clan. They said if left alive she would hunt and try to kill me and my parents for the rest of eternity because I am the superior witch now. She thinks I stole her birth right, but mother said she realized a long time ago that her sister was not to be the superior witch that I had been the chosen one all along. There was nothing else to be done under the circumstances. I was not in attendance for the killing. I didn't want to witness that terrible event although I hated her for what she had done. She helped murder my parents.

On the other hand I am so happy now that my parents are here to teach me how to use my powers wisely for the good of all as it was always meant to be.

"There you are. I've been searching the house for you." say's Marcus out of nowhere bringing me out of my wool gathering. Strange I was so deep in thought I didn't since him walk in.

"My sexy lawman has busted me." I purr in a teasing way as he walks towards me in his sensuous manly strut that only he could pull off.

"Yes, I have a surprise for you." He says as he reaches me, pulling me in for a kiss. Umm his lips are scrumptious. Will I ever tire of his sweet unbelievably sexy and what I compare to, 'Elvis lips' all fleshy, and pouty, and so magnificent. He nibbles on my bottom lip with his teeth.

I hope not baby, because I'll never tire of yours. He whispers on our Eternalmate only line, and it is amazing to have this kind of intimacy as he pulls me in closer to his body. Umm did you say Elvis lips?

Uh huh.

That's new, when did you start describing them like that?

A while ago, I usually try to hide it around you.

"Oh I see, hmm, you mean the guy who sings, 'Jail House Rock?" he asks out loud this time.

"Leave it to a cop to think of that song first." I say, snickering then add, "He also sang 'Love Me Tender."

"Isn't he dead, - as in not coming back, dead?"

"Yes, he's dead as far as what I've been told although many people think he faked his death to get out of the lime light, but I'll always remember those pouty lips."

"I don't think I like the thought of that." He stiffens.

"Jealous of a dead man, Marcus?"

"A little."

I giggle, "Don't be he's dead, I think. By the way did you mention a surprise?"

"Yes I did, come with me," he takes my hand and pulls me toward the door.

"Where are we going?"

"You'll find out in a minute. Close your eyes, and keep them shut until I say to open them," he say's leading me down a path of stones and through a grove of trees from what it feels like, as I brush against a leafy branch and the long wild grass on each side tickles my bare legs.

We walk for a while and I'm about to ask how much longer when he stops me.

"Open your eyes, Issy," he whispers in my right ear in a voice that makes my skin tingle and my lower stomach muscles tighten. I open my eyes and can't believe what's there. Tears fill my eyes and I am speechless, simply speechless. "Well, say something... do you like it?"

"This is what you've been doing all this time when you leave?"

"Yes." His voice cracks.

"For me?" I ask, crossing my hands over my heart. I can't believe he built me a cabin. I'm touched. No one's ever done anything like this for me before.

"Of course for you."

"But why?"

"Because I love you, Issy. You're my Eternalmate, and I would do anything to make you happy."

"I love you too."

"There's more."

"More? This is more than I ever imagined."

He takes my hand pulling me along the path alongside the cabin where there are beautiful flowers everywhere. My eyes fill with tears. Why did he build me a cabin? He stops sliding out of my way so that I could discover what's ahead of us. A spectacular gazebo with flowers of all the colors of a rainbow threaded throughout.

I stare up at him in awe eyes filling with tears.

"This is where we will be married tomorrow. And afterwards it is your garden where I will teach you how to tend the dirt, and all of the plants or anything else you choose to plant here. This way your thumb will be green too." He grins.

I pant, overcome with joy.

"The cabin I'm guessing is what you expected the first time I brought you here. I thought you might want a place to come and relax alone to read or possibly some time to yourself away from the children…" he peers at me holding his breath and I discover the hope in his eyes, "or whatever you'd like to use the space for. Perhaps I was silly to think you …"

"You are the kindest man, Marcus." I take hold of his face so I can peer straight into his eyes. "Don't you ever forget that? I'm the happiest woman in the world since meeting you. I love all of it, the cabin, the gazebo, the gardens and most of all my incredibly adorable teacher. And in case you were hinting around about having children, the answer is yes… I want children and I want to start as soon as possible."

"I was hoping you'd say that. What do ya say we…." he purrs, with a gleam of mischief in his blue eyes.

"Well, there is a cabin right …" I try to say pointing at said cabin, but he doesn't let me finish.

"Now you're thinking."

"How did I get so lucky as to find you, Marcus?"

"Baby you falling into the Shitkick bar was the luckiest day of my life," he says, picking me up and heading towards the back door of the cabin.

"What about my parents?"

"We're loud, but not that loud. They're a half a mile away." he says with a chuckle.

"Oh, but don't you think we should wait until after the wedding?"

"Nope, my plan for tomorrow you'll discover after the ceremony. Besides, I want to spend our last night before the wedding, and all the rest of our families get here, alone, the two of us in the cabin. I bought all your favorites, champagne, strawberries, chocolate…"

"Say no more." I giggle, as our lips come together happy beyond belief.

The end

Thank you for reading Lover's Salvation the second book in The Hemocil Society. I hope you fell in love with all the characters as I did. If you've not read the first in the series Lover's Curse you'll want to check it out too. Lover's Refuge the third in this series will be out this winter 2015 if everything goes as planned. Thank you again and happy reading. Ps write me a line and tell me what you think. loverscurserm@yahoo.com. also check out my author page on Amazon.com/author/ruthielmanier and write me a review. It would be much appreciated.

About the Author

Ruthie L Manier

Hi I'm Ruthie, and I'm happy you took the time to read my book. I Live and work In Skagit County, Washington. I've been married for almost thirty years to a man I adore. We are the parents of four adult children; two daughters, and two sons. We currently have been blessed with four grandchildren, with one on the way. We have a golden retriever named Moses, (Moe) that is fifteen years old, and we love him as though he is blood. My favorite things to do when I have free time are; dressing up like the characters from my favorite books, pirates, witches, vampires, damsels in distress, and acting out the parts. (Just kidding) Spending time with my family and friends is at the top of my list, and camping or any kind of outside physical activities would be next. But most of all, I enjoy writing or reading a book that is so good it sets my mind free, and makes it wander to new places and believe in things that are completely unbelievable...

CPSIA information can be obtained
at www.ICGtesting.com
Printed in the USA
LVOW01s2124011115
460683LV00009B/84/P

9 781515 096924